Chiefdom of the Marshes

By

John Williamson

Copyright ©2021 John Williamson
all rights reserved
ISBN: 9798476465782

Note to readers

This book is written with an adult audience in mind and does contain some swearing and violence for the purposes of authenticity.

Every effort has been made to make the detail and description as accurate to the era as our knowledge allows, but in such a distant time, our understanding is almost entirely dependant upon the admirable work of generations of archaeologists, and as such, much has to be supposition.

Acknowledgements

As previously mentioned, much is owed to the work of archaeologists, excavators and historians, over the course of many decades, but I feel special mention should be given to the work at Must Farm and Flag Fen. It was a childhood visit to the Flag Fen site, when it was in its infancy, that first instilled a fascination in the era. The story itself was also inspired by their excavations, specifically the causeway and related artefacts.

As ever I dedicate this book to my wife Marie and my children; Samantha, Aidan, Bethany and Megan, who are my constant inspiration for all that I do.

I would also like to thank you, my readers, for taking the time to follow my work and hope you'll read on with me as 'The Marshes' series continues. If you haven't already, why not search out 'Rib Bone Jack,' Set during the Napoleonic wars, and 'Legacy of the Rhino,' set after the first global revolution, in 2035.

Chapter 1

Not even the greatest seers and mystics of the time could have foretold the changes blowing on the wind, as it drifted the trader's boat along the vast winding river, which linked the many villages of the marshes.

As it passed, the faces of children peered through the imposing reeds of the river margins, signalled the proximity to the next village, on the traders route.

The boat was in itself of greater value than the combined possessions of many of the communities it visited, its plank structure and considerable cargo capacity making its owner a rich man, before any trade was even considered.

As the boat approached the narrow channel, which broke off from the main river, the youngest and leanest of the three men on board, guided the vessel away from the reeds with a long oar. A second, heavily build young man wrapped the single ox hide sail as it began to drag on the tops of the reeds.

Not a word was spoken. Each of the three knew what was required of him. The two young men tended to the operating of the boat. Each taking to one of the oversized oars as they reached the open water ahead of them, while the older man moved to the bow, presenting himself, almost theatrically as they approached the first of the two villages, which lived by the reed encircled lake.

With every stroke of the oars, more people gathered, each of them excited to see the goods available to trade.

"Maldred," a man of about forty called in welcome, from the water's edge.

"Thane Elric," the trader called back, extending his arms as if greeting the dearest of friends.

Everything about Maldred was for show. Despite the heat of high summer, he insisted upon wearing a silver wolf fur; a luxurious item from far beyond the great sea. His hair and full beard were greying, matching the wolf fur in colour, perfectly. As he stood proudly at the bow of his boat, he rested his hand on the perfectly fashioned bronze axe, a tool that had clearly never been used.

There was a gaggle of excitement as the villagers pulled the boat into moor. Men, women and children alike, bubbling and whispering as they took first sight of the goods on board.

A family was herding six sheep into a wooden pen, for Maldred's attention, while three cart wheels were frantically rolled out for display. "Very impressive," Maldred said patronisingly as he passed, but being careful not to show too much interest in the villager's trading goods.

"Come, we have much to eat," Elric announced, beckoning Maldred to follow him to his roundhouse.

"Lind," Maldred called back to the ship, accompanied by an instructive nod. That was all the instruction needed for Maldred's son to tie the hands of the young man, securing him to the frame of the boat. "Come, my boy, there's someone you need to meet."

Elric glanced at Maldred enquiringly, unsure of whom Maldred spoke.

"Your wise seer, of course. If only such knowledge could be traded. Your village would be rich in deed," Maldred explained.

Elric smiled politely, but did not comment. Instead he pointed to a woman with a basket on her shoulder, and then to his hut, requiring her to deliver it to his roundhouse.

Maldred held his stomach, assuming the eel basket to represent his meal. "May I request something of the land, rather than the water. I'm sure if I eat another fish I'll sprout fins."

"Of course. I'll have something killed immediately," Elric agreed, his voice failing to hide his offence and disappointment.

"A vision of beauty, as ever," Maldred declared as Elric's wife stood in the glow of the fire, stirring a large pot.

"I hope you're as generous in your trade as you are your compliments," Isena replied with a welcoming smile. "How your son has grown," she added as Lind ducked his head to enter the house, both his height and general size being striking.

"I fear it's been too long since our last visit," Maldred said in a more serious tone, suggesting all was not well in his world.

"Please, Sit Lind," Isena insisted, guiding the young man to one of the five fur draped logs, which surrounded the central fire. "We have stew for now, and freshly baked bread, and a whole sheep for tonight." Before Maldred could protest, Isena began to scoop a bowl full of the eel based dish.

Maldred smiled politely, before prodding one of the floating lumps in his bowl, in the hope of identifying it.

"Did you see our wheels on your way in," Elric began enthusiastically. "Eldwan and his sons have found new sources for the perfect timber."

"They are craftsmen," Maldred agreed sombrely. "Ten winters ago I'd have happily loaded my vessel with Eldwan's wheels... now they just take too much space for their value... Everyone's making them these days." Maldred gestured to Lind to sample the stew, as he tentatively supped from his spoon. "Do you still have no crop land?"

"A little, some times. When the spirits of the river allow it," Elric replied guardedly. "What they take from us in one manner, they return richly in the fruits of the water."

"Quite so, my friend," Maldred agreed, once more prodding the pieces of fish in his bowl, contemplating methods of politely rejecting the meal.

"We have sheep. The sheep do wonders in the marshes, for as long as we can keep them from the river," Elric suggested optimistically.

Maldred shook his head. "I'm sorry, I should have explained upon my arrival, I don't trade in such things any more... Many a summer and winter I have travelled with my boat weighed down with timber and rotting meat. Not any more."

"Then what do you trade," Isena asked.

"Sweat. Labour. Hungry souls."

Elric cast such an enquiring look as to not require words.

"Just imagine Elric, imagine every days work you have ever done, every day you will ever do. Every demeaning task that's below you place in the world, done for you."

"Slaves?" Isena interrupted with disgust.

"As I said, dear lady, hungry souls... See that lad out there, he's worth a boat load of cart wheels, or half the sheep in your marsh," Maldred said with an edge to his voice.

"Does he not have a family he should be working for, or a village to which he belongs?" Isena argued, to Elric's silent disapproval.

"That's the wonder of it, dear lady... Imagine a family facing a winter with little food and no wealth. What hope have they of seeing the breaking of buds in spring, without loss?" Maldred flicked his finger to Lind, instructing him to present the contents of a tightly wrapped bear fur. "For one member of that roundhouse to be surrendered, they all live, that is a very good price, you'll surely agree."

Lind unrolled the skin to expose it's rich contents. A row of perfectly fashioned, bronze spearheads and a leather pouch, full of razor sharp arrowheads were the first items to come into view, followed by three equally immaculate axeheads. "A family would live well with these alone," Maldred said as Lind paused the opening of the roll, in what was a piece of rehearsed and well practised theatre.

Lind continued to unroll the hide, revealing eight perfectly round, brightly coloured green stones, three decorated broaches and detailed stone carving of a wolf. "That's the price, that's the worth of one of your young men, so never think you're poor."

Elric and Isena made eye contact, both chilled and shocked by what was being suggested. "I'm afraid Maldred, we're not going to be able to trade today," Elric declared, his focus fixed on the wealth of goods on offer. "Please, stay as our guest tonight, just the same."

"Here he is," Maldred suddenly announced, with a voice contrastingly full of joy. "This is the man I've been telling you about." He was staring through the open doorway, watching as an old man approached, bent over and propped up by a many times twisted stick.

Lind watched as the old man entered the house, his crippled stature such that to look up at them was a painful exercise. "This, my boy is the wisest man you'll ever meet. A man able to talk to the spirits," Maldred explained, bowing as the old man shuffled past. "This is my son, Lind."

The old man ignored his words completely, instead making his way to the fire. He wore a single tatty cloth gown, which was dirty, to such an extent that he may have easily owned nothing else. "Da?" Lind said in disappointed awe, at the man his father spoke so highly of.

"You would have been just a child on your last visit. Your time would have been taken with play." Isena's words were tailored to justify Lind's poorly shrouded amusement at the little old man.

The old man stood dangerously close to the fire and slowly unfolded a small leather pouch. Maldred slapped Lind's knee to gain his full attention as the old man took a pinch of the dust like substance in the pouch and threw it into the flames. For just a second the flames changes in both colour and shape, rising higher and hissing, before returning to their original state.

The old man turned, twisting his head up to fix an unnerving stare upon Maldred. "Do you have something for me?" He demanded, his voice harsh and unforgiving.

"Of course. Dried the way you told me to."

The old man snatched the woven cloth from Maldred's hand and unfolded it next to the dust. He picked through the tiny multicoloured fungi, first sniffing, then touching them on the tip of his tongue. "Hmm," he uttered, folding both parcels and gripping them in the palm of his hand, before turning for the door.

"Are you not going to tell us what you saw in the flames, wise one?" Maldred tentatively asked as the old man made his way to the door.

"Knowledge can be a destructive thing. Knowledge of the future only brings a man's troubles to meet him... Do you still want to know?" The old man scowled as he asked the question, his thinning, long white hair partially obscuring his face as he awaited Maldred's answer.

"Yes, wise one. A man needs to see his path."

"Hmm... Three men visit us today, with three very different paths," the old man began, glaring once more at Maldred, his behaviour sufficiently out of the ordinary to gain even Elric's attention.

The old man drew three lines in the dirt with his stick, before drawing across one of the lines. "One path will be done within seven suns."

Maldred didn't speak. He didn't react at all, except for the fact that he turned the palest shade of white. He looked to Isena, who was breaking open a freshly baked loaf. "That would be most welcome," he uttered, finally ending the atmosphere of tense silence.

Nobody even noticed the old man leave. His words had done their damage. Maldred had nothing more to say on the matter, despite the fact that little else occupied his mind.

"Would you be wanting to stay, Maldred?" Isena asked. "Or were you hoping to cross the lake to our neighbours, before darkness?"

"I fear we need to be back on the river," Maldred uttered, gazing deep into his stew.

Elric studied him. The old man had cast doubt deep into his soul, but he felt sure there was more to it than that. "He's not always right, you know," Elric suggested, in the hope of offering some comfort.

"I know. That's not all of it though," Maldred uttered, once more fixing his vision on the bowl in front of him.

"Da, I thought we'd agreed not to say," Lind interrupted.

"Boy, I've been visiting these people since before you were thought of. We need to be thinking of running now, not trade."

Isena sat beside Elric, clutching a piece of the bread, anticipating bad news. "What is it, Maldred?" she asked, as Elric discretely gripped her hand.

"Stromgalee!" he blurted, as if daring himself to say the name.

"Who told you this. Surely he crossed the great sea. Why would he be back?"

"Why did you wait until now to tell us?" Isena interrupted angrily, before Maldred could answer Elric's question.

"Why scare the trade?" Lind said with a grin.

"There's nothing knowing will do to help you... He might sail straight past," Maldred suggested.

"And if he doesn't?" Isena demanded with increasing anger.

"Give him what he wants. He doesn't claim to be a raider. He asks for gratitude for his visit. He'll settle for one precious item of his choosing, but if it's not given, he'll take everything else and burn what he can't carry on his boats."

"Look around you, Maldred. What do we have?" she demanded.

"This would satisfy him," Maldred tentatively and nervously suggested, tapping his finger on the roll of goods.

Elric scowled at him, no longer knowing what to believe, while Isena stood and walked out without speaking another word, convinced that Maldred's story was designed solely to convince them to sell someone into slavery.

"Andura," she called, seeing her daughter at Maldred's boat, talking to the slave. "Come away from there, now."

Andura was of a mind to argue, as was often the case, but for the sight of tears rolling down her mother's face. "What is it mother," she asked. "Is there no trade to be had."

"No, no trade, but that's not what makes me angry. It's the lies and nastiness a man will use to increase his wealth." Isena was raging. Her tears were not to be mistaken for weakness. The tribe of her birth were renowned for their fearsome nature, and she was no exception.

"What was said, Mother? Was it about the raids?"

Isena almost instantly composed herself, fixing an enquiring stare upon her daughter. "What do you know?"

"Vintnor told me. Some sort of warlord." She looked back at the slave, as if to introduce him to Isena, her eyes sparkling as if taken by the muscular young man, who sat tied to the hull of the boat.

Isena glanced back to the roundhouse, before marching over to Maldred's boat with vigour and purpose. "What is it you've seen?"

Vintnor sat, crouched, lowering his head to demonstrate respect. "The villages, lady? Burning!"

"Who? Why?"

"Stromgalee," he replied, still with his head lowered, his long brown hair cloaking his face.

Isena looked back at the roundhouse. Maldred and Lind were leaving, being politely escorted by Elric.

"Who is Stromgalee, Mother?" Andura asked with increasing concern as her mother lost every bit of colour from her flesh, at the very mention of the name.

Isena ignored her, instead turning back to Vintnor. "Where was this?" she demanded.

"Towards the resting sun," he replied. "Three days and nights ago."

Isena gripped Andura's hand, conveying her absolute fear. "So he could be just as easily on the river now."

"Mother, who is Stromgalee?"

Isena looked her deep into the eyes, considering the question and the wisdom of answering honestly. "You're not to worry," she insisted, leading Andura away from the boat, and from Vintnor. She gripped her daughter's hand tightly, purposefully, to stop her hand from shaking.

"Mother?" Andura snapped, the one angrily placed word, designed to achieve an informative response.

"Let's walk the eel traps," Isena agreed, the eel traps being stacked at the far end of the village, drying in the late afternoon sun. Significantly, they were entirely unattended and beyond the earshot of the villagers. "Stromgalee was a trader, much like Maldred. He and his father ran a boat each and had men under their command. Not the nicest people, but not to be feared either."

"So, what happened? Why would they burn villages?"

"When the father died, the son took a new course... He found he could take without giving. To inflict his might over on those weaker than himself. He began to gather the worst, the faithless, the outcasts, those who would serve him without question. His evil ways were reward enough for them."

"Will they come here, Mother," Andura asked with a tear in her eye and a falter in her voice.

"We will make a gift to the water spirits, to guide their boats from our village, and another on the night of the round moon. Surely the spirits could never favour such beasts," Isena said, to reassure her daughter, but her words lacked conviction. "Should he come, you are to run... Hide in the marshes, until it is safe."

"No Mother, not without you, without everyone."

"You'll do as you are told. Stromgalee seeks property, possessions, items of value. You are a young woman now, and a Thane's daughter. In the eyes of his kind, that is your worth." Isena gripped her hand with both of hers, as if begging her to listen. "Promise me you'll hide, should he come."

Andura stared back at her. She knew it was the wrong time to revive the old argument, but Isena's words inflamed her disapproval of the marriage, which had been arranged for her with the Thane's son, in the neighbouring village.

She pulled her hand away and wiped away a solitary tear. "Yet you plan to sell me off to Norsea! Am I not just property?"

"We will not be discussing this now, not again," Isena snapped, her voice contrastingly sharp to before. "Would you rather marry one of them?" she asked, lowering her voice as two skinny youngsters rowed into view, in log boats.

"I would choose!"

"Dalric of Norsea is a fine young man... You are a Thane's daughter, you have responsibilities."

"The Thane of eight roundhouses, that's Father's greatness, and what does he do with his days. He cuts trees, shovels shit, guts fish, just the same as everyone else. What's the cursed point!" In her rage, she hurried across the village, where the rest of the villagers had gathered, watching in confusion as Maldred and his son were boarding there boat, empty handed.

Her tantrums had been regular, since the announcement of her planned marriage, and so her troubled state was noticed by no one, with the exception of the young slave, Vintnor. He was in the eyes of those present, all but invisible. So much so that when the two fixed an all telling stare across the crowd, nobody even noticed.

Chapter 2

Maldred returned to his boat in a troubled state. His mind was so occupied by the old man's prophecy, that he couldn't concentrate on matters of trade. He did his best to leave in a polite manner, but the haste with which he returned to his boat confused and worried the villagers, and the fact that he decided not to visit the larger village of Norsea, across the lake, highlighted the fact that something was drastically amiss.

Vintnor watched as Maldred awkwardly pushed the boat away from the mooring, with one of the oars. Everything seemed wrong; Maldred's flustered state and the cluster of people anxiously waiting at the Norsea mooring, only half a mile across the lake. "Not so good then?" Vintnor said cheerfully, holding his tied hands out to be released.

"Leave him tied," Maldred growled dryly and coldly, prompting Vintnor to sit back down on a pile hides, oblivious to the old man's prophesy.

Lind hurriedly pushed the boat along, bedding the oar into the shallow mud of the lake margins, while Maldred guided the boat around a network of fish traps, which lurked an inch below the surface. Both men worked in complete silence, ignoring the onlookers on the bank; ignoring each other even.

As they entered the narrow channel, leading to the river, a boy of no more than six appeared through the reeds. "Where are you going, boatmen," he called. "Don't you want our things."

Maldred fixed the saddest gaze upon the boy, but still did not speak. He reached into the bottom of the boat and rummaged amongst rope and flagons, eventually producing a small wooden axe, fashioned by his own hand. He looked at it deeply. It would normally have been a gift for the child of a Thane or a Chief, but as he threw it to the boy, in his own mind it felt to him like some token of an apology to the entire village.

"Thanks boatman," the boy giggled with delight, but Maldreds stone cold, miserable expression did not change.

As the wide open river appeared, Maldred at last spoke. He nudged Lind and pointed to the blood red sun as it began to lower itself behind the wall of reeds, which lined the river margins. "Does that not tell us what has to be done," he whispered.

"You'd see us peasants," Lind complained, looking back at Vintnor with agitation.

"I'd see us live. Both of us," Maldred argued.

"Would you not have me take my place on the oar, master?" Vintnor asked, becoming concerned by the morbid atmosphere and the fact that the oars were not actually being used properly, nor the sail unfolded.

"Hold your tongue, boy," Maldred snapped, his attention entirely captivated by the setting sun. "The greatest of the spirits has a message for us," he sighed quietly.

The river was busy. Log boaters were returning to their villages for the night, loaded with the fruits of their days hunting and foraging. A patch of reed was being cut on the far shore, for roundhouse roofs, allowing the sun to shine through so much clearer.

Maldred watched the rippling of the water, reflecting back the redness of the setting sun with such striking beauty that he took it as a sign; a request even. "It must be now, before the greatest of the spirits," Maldred blurted, with a sudden burst of energy.

Vintnor looked on, baffled, but increasingly concerned by what he was hearing. Suddenly, Lind grabbed him by the arm and yanked him to the side of the boat, forcing his head to the edge, so as to rest his neck on the side.

"I will row. Let me row," Vintnor pleaded, in a state of panic, as he realised he was to be sacrificed.

Maldred handed Lind an ornately decorated knife. "You must do your part too. A gift from us both." Those were the words that confirmed beyond all doubt in Vintnor's mind that he was about to die.

For just a few seconds he felt the pressure on his neck ease, as Lind reached out to receive the knife. Lind was strong, Stronger that Vintnor, but at that moment the balance was on his side. He placed his left foot hard into a flagon of corn and pushed hard, not to escape, but to turn. As he rolled, he saw Maldred, clutching his pristine axe, poised to strike, while Lind grabbed at the ceremonial knife, missing as he struggled to contain his intended victim.

The tussle was such that Maldred couldn't strike a safe blow, without hitting Lind. He stood, with his axe drawn back, waiting for a clear shot.

"People are watching, Father," Lind gasped as he began to force Vintnor's head back to the side of the boat.

"Let them watch. He's ours to do with as we please."

"Why are you doing this," Vintnor gasped, once more forcing Lind aside, and spoiling Maldred's shot in the process.

"The spirits demand it, now meet your fate like a man," Maldred snarled, swiping at Vintnor's thigh as he turned.

The first contact from Maldred's blade, seemed to focus Vintnor's mind. He brought his knee forwards vigorously, striking Lind in the groin, inspiring him to release his grip, just for a second. In that second he lurched forwards, propelling himself into the water, before Maldred could strike a second blow.

"This axe to the man that catches him," Maldred shouted to two reed cutters, working on the far shore.

Lind scrambled to his feet, snatching at a bundle of spears, frantically untying their binding. "He's gone under. The cursed sod's gone under," Maldred said in a more relaxed, relieved tone, realising that Vintnor's hands were still firmly tied.

The water gradually stilled, while Lind stood with a ready spear, prepared for the ever decreasing chance of Vintnor reappearing.

"A gift to the water spirits, as it turns out," Maldred uttered, only slightly concerned that such a great sacrifice had been made to the wrong deity.

As those words left his mouth, a sudden splash seized their attention, caused by Vintnor, springing to the surface, swimming frantically for the bank; his hands untied.

"Kill him. You must kill him," Maldred shouted, whilst grabbing at an oar, to propel the boat to the reed engulfed river margin. Lind stood at the bow, studying his target, absorbing his ever movement, to be sure of a perfect kill. He drew back his heavily muscled arm and twisted his body with it, to allow every muscle to play its part.

It was a matter of luck, rather than judgement, that Vintnor's body was at a sharp angle in the water at the moment the spear slid along his back, but still the sharpened bronze head sliced deep. With every stretch of his arm, the wound opened, making swimming both agonising and impractical. He floundered for a second, looking back to see Lind, armed with a second spear and the boat approaching fast.

Lind was an accomplished spearsman, at a range in which he could not miss. To Vintnor, the sight of Lind drawing back his spear arm represented impending death. To dive was no escape, but it was an instinctive reaction to buy a few seconds.

Two men in a log boat deliberately redirected themselves across the river as the water once more stilled. "Is the offer of the axe open to us?" the older and rougher of the two poorly groomed fishermen called.

"If you get him before my son," Maldred replied, confident of his son's skill with a spear.

The redness of the setting sun had all but gone from the water, leaving its surface dark and forbidding. A sudden explosion from the margins, breaking the water surface with dramatic effect, before it rained back down, exposing the head and shoulders of Vintnor, his arm and empty hand held above his head.

Maldred's attention was drawn by the sound of Lind's spear, clattering onto the deck. He stood, sideways on, motionless, expressionless, as his body slowly leant backwards, splashing into the water, already dead from the spear, which had passed through his chest, its bronze point protruding from his back.

"Kill the wretch... Kill him," Maldred shouted frantically to the two in the log boat. "Kill the bastard." Then after, he stared into the water, as his son slowly sank from sight.

The two fishermen quite purposefully and hurriedly paddled back into the main flow of the river, while Maldred fell to his knees, uttering words to any deity that might choose to listen. Only as they were some distance away, did Maldred notice them missing. "My boat and all its contents for that slave... Everything I have, for his dead corpse," he sobbed, hanging his arms over the side, as if desperately reaching for something entirely out of reach.

"That spear was guided by powerful spirits, boatman... He's your problem," the older of the fishermen called, as he rowed all the faster, for his fear.

Chapter 3

Vintnor had dragged himself only a few yards from the river, through the waterlogged reed beds, before passing out. He had rolled and struggled his way through a thick soup of near black mud, on the river margin, which have served to slow his bleeding.

He laid there for most of the night, his mind empty of thoughts and his body at the mercy of the water spirits. It was as if he had taken a long blink, or just had a very vivid dream, as he woke to the first light of a mid summer dawn. His vision was clouded by the mud, caked around his eyes. The sensation of his leg being pushed and prodded, seemed like the continuation a dream. Only the snorting and grunting of the boar, which was considering his value as a meal, startled him to life.

He kicked with his feet, while trying to scramble through the waterlogged reeds. Both the injury to his thigh and his back, grabbed him with the sharpest of pains, confirming every detail he could remember to be real.

The boar took two steps back, before reasserting itself. Caked in drying mud and still smelling of blood; Vintnor was, in the eyes of the boar, an injured animal, ripe for the kill. It snorted as if to challenge him, before charging forwards with its tusks low to the ground.

It was a lucky shot with his foot, that allowed Vintnor to deflect the animal's charge, but in no way was the boar discouraged. It immediately turned about, lining him up for a more determined attack.

A single willow sapling represented the only object around him that wasn't reeds. He clutched it with his right arm and pulled, in the hope of dragging himself to his feet, but as he did so it came out by its roots.

His first instinct was to throw it away in disgust, and he would have done, if the boar hadn't charged a second later. In stead he lashed at its face, roaring loudly as he gathered all his remaining strength and energy, to see off the determined beast. Only briefly did he stand fully upright, before his injured thigh dropped him back to his knees, but it was enough to present the boar with an adversary it considered dangerous.

Vintnor knelt in the saturated moss, listening to the retreating boar as it rustled through the reeds. The sound only slowly faded, keeping his nerves on edge. He could hear water birds on the river behind, indicating that he was dangerously close to the busy waterway.

He lifted his tunic, enough to inspect his thigh wound. It was caked in a blend of mud and blood, and sore to the touch, enough to make him wince with the pain. He squeezed the water from a handful of clean moss and hurriedly wiped the wound, to reveal a bruised patch, surrounding a darkened, four inch long gash. The motion of wiping the mud away was enough to pull on the spear wound, on his back; a wound he could not reach or even see.

The distant sound of movement in the reeds ahead brought him, awkwardly to his feet. The grunting of a hog, suggested the boar's return, yet it's distressed pitch felt like something more ominous.

With no view of his surroundings, in any direction, Vintnor once more armed himself with the willow sapling. It was a pathetic weapon, but he felt armed; it was something rather than nothing. He stood, lurched to one side like an injured animal, his wounds not allowing his to stand upright comfortably.

Again the boar grunted; close this time, yet not in sight. He drew the sapling back, in preparation to strike. Splashing and the breaking of reeds, came a second before the boar's frantic appearance only a few feet away. This time, far from attacking, the animal changed course, running to his side.

With the boar passed, the sound of breaking reeds continued. He looked back to where the boar had run from, to see a hefty young man, running with a ready spear.

Their vision locked. The young man stopped, his face blank as he considered what he was seeing, and what he should do about it. Vintnor studied his face. He was confused, scared even, which he saw as a danger. Vintnor slowly lowered the sapling, as a symbolic gesture, hoping to calm him. Still neither man blinked.

"I think I might need help," Vintnor uttered as he collapsed into the water, neither unconscious, nor able to move without assistance.

"What is it, Dugan?" Andura asked the young man as he hurried towards the Thane's roundhouse.

"I've found him, lady. I've, I've found him," Dugan spluttered excitedly, his weak mind being clear with every word.

"Who have you found?"

"The spear man. The one. The one they're looking for."

Andura grabbed him by the arm, as he attempted to continue to the Thane's roundhouse, where Maldred had spent the night raging and grieving in equal measure. "First tell me," she began, with a mesmerising smile. "How did you catch such a man." As she spoke, she guided him from sight, behind a stack of reeds.

Dugan thought about her question for a prolonged period of time, before answering, "he just laid there," whilst making a flopping gesture with his arms.

"Was he hurt?" Andura asked with poorly masked concern.

Dugan nodded vigorously, overwhelmed by the interest she was suddenly taking in him.

"Must tell Thane Elric and trader Maldred," he blurted as he attempted to pass her.

"Not yet, Dugan," she insisted, stepping fully in his path. Pressing her chest to his. "I fear it is more than poor Maldred could cope with… Why don't you take me to him and we can keep him safe, until my father can decide what to do."

Dugan looked at her blankly; confused and conflicted by what she was suggesting. Once more he attempted to push his way past her, and once more she pushed her considerable breasts to his chest, more obviously deliberate this time. "Take me to him. You'll be the hero of the village. You see," she said as his face slowly filled with delight, not for her words, but her proximity. "Will you take me to him?" she asked as she took his wrist in her hand and slowly guided his hand beneath her top and up, until it was gripping her breast.

Dugan nodded. Bright red in the face, and in such a state of bewilderment that he could neither have refused her nor attempted to take the situation any further.

They left unseen. The search for Vintnor had already begun, leaving the village all but empty. Maldred had said little of Vintnor's wounds, in an attempt to portray himself in a favourable light, to Elric. As such it had been assumed that he had run through the night, into the woodlands, beyond the marsh.

Dugan bounded forwards, following his own tracks, through the reeds. He was entirely under her spell, his feeble mind unable to refuse her. "It's this way. By the river," he gushed, overwhelmed with delight.

"There he is," Andura replied, suddenly running ahead, to meet the young man who had so fascinated her, the day before. He lay only a couple of yards from where Dugan had left him, conscious enough to recognise her and smile with joy, as a result.

He was soaked, he had been for much of the night, and his hands shook, to prove it. "I know a place," she said, pulling him to his feet. "Are you going to help?" she snapped at Dugan.

"Shouldn't we take him to the village?" Dugan replied, his concerns once more returning.

"It's a sacred place. A fertile place," she whispered to him, as if it were a secret she was sharing only with him. She stroked his hand briefly, before transferring Vintnor's weight to him. "I don't have your great strength," she declared, rubbing his quite flabby arm.

It was an irregular shaped area of raised ground, less than the area of a roundhouse. High and dry enough to grow grass, rather than reeds, and entirely unexplained. The elders of the two villages had always said it to be an alter to the water spirits. In times of flood, gifts and small sacrifices were placed there, in the hope of holding back the high waters; offerings that were invariable washed away by flood water.

Vintnor laid for some time, on the dry bank, watched over by Dugan, while Andura went off in search of Eleena, the granddaughter of the elderly seer. She was a capable healer and a trusted friend.

While he waiting, Vintnor attempted to explain his actions on the river, to Dugan, but quickly came to the conclusion that he was a simpleton and closed his eyes, pretending to be asleep, rather than continue the one sided conversation.

It was some time later, before Andura returned, accompanied by the young woman, in her early twenties, with long, bright orange hair. At first Vintnor didn't speak. He quite obviously looked her over, from head to toe, his eyes drawn to the three inches or so, of mud on the hem of her long, light blue dress. "I'm sorry for the trouble," he said, as he fixed his attention on her heavily freckled face.

"You're a trouble, right enough," she said, as she knelt beside him, to inspect the wound on his back.

"They were trying to kill me. You must understand, it was what I had to do," he pleaded with both women.

"My father has already worked it out... The seer's prophecy. One of the three of you was to die. They wanted to make sure it was you," Andura explained.

"You have powerful spirits on your side," Eleena added, as she dabbed his wound with a stinking moss poultice.

"Spirits or not, my father will give you back to Maldred," Andura whispered, so as to avoid Dugan's ears. "It's just the way of him, it's what he'll do."

Vintnor winced with pain as Eleena pressed the poultice firmly on the wound, causing its herbal contents to leach into the wound. "It's his duty. I'm Maldred's property," Vintnor said, gritting his teeth as the concoction stung deep into the open gash.

"We can hide you for a while, but Maldred isn't going to give up," Andura uttered, with one eye on Dugan, whom she knew would eventually tell someone. "How'd you get to be a slave anyway," she asked with frustration, as if it were a lifestyle choice. "Were you born to it?"

"No, I wasn't born a slave," he said with a wry smile, as memories from an earlier life entered his head. "I was like you. A hunter in fact, and a bloody good one, but our village couldn't live on hunting alone... When the crops failed, we knew we weren't likely to all see the season of the breaking buds. I was the eldest of six children. We had the most to lose, so when Maldred made his offer, I put myself forward... He never said anything about sacrifices, though."

"That's all very brave and good, but it won't save you from Maldred's axe," Eleena said without sympathy. "Do you think you can walk far, on this leg?" she asked as she lifted his tunic to inspect the thigh wound.

"Far, maybe, but not very fast. Your people are looking for me, aren't they?"

Eleena did not answer. She looked to Andura with a telling eye. "An offering needs to be made. You've brought him to a sacred place, but you must make a gift, else the spirits of the water will surely take him as your offering."

Andura drew from her belt, a small knife, which she carried constantly. "It was a gift from my father," she said tentatively, holding the knife in front of her. Her eyes welled at the thought of its loss, as she looked to Eleena for instruction.

"Break it and gently place it in the water," Eleena explained as she laid two pieces of wood side by side, to break the knife on. "And you need to say the words," she added, tapping the logs to hurry her up.

Andura remembered the many waterside offerings she had witnessed, since her early childhood. She placed a third piece of wood across the middle of the knife and hit it forcefully with her palm, breaking the blade from the handle. "I willingly and deliberately make you this gift, in the hope you will watch over and protect this man from harm." As she recited the words, she knelt at the water's edge and lowered the two pieces into the water, gently and slowly, as if she were placing them in someone's hand.

"Now we need to go," Eleena said coldly and sharply. "You need to follow the hunter's axe, as soon as darkness falls," she added, drawing a pattern of stars in a bare patch of earth. "Don't stop until you are far from this place. You have no friends here." Eleena's words were harsh and abrupt, reflecting her own fear of the trouble he might yet cause.

Vintnor looked to Andura, for kinder words, or even a benevolent smile, but Andura turned her head away, understanding at last the risk she had taken.

"And you, Dugan. Understand that if just one word of this is repeated, I will instruct a dozen harvest mice to gnaw off your tiny dick, while you sleep." Eleena kept a perfectly straight face as she made the threat, while both Vintnor and Andura struggled to hide their amusement, lightening the otherwise tense situation between them.

Dugan looked to his feet. He had a healthy respect for Eleena. Her skill with herbs and medicines, combined with her being the granddaughter of the seer, had caused many a tongue to whisper of her powers. His silence was assured, for a time, at least.

Chapter 4

It was the first time Maldred had left the Thane's roundhouse, since his arrival in the village, the night before. He stood shoulder to shoulder with Elric and Isena, appearing as equals, as they stood to greet Consada, Thane of Norsea.

Consada stood proudly at the front of the largest log boat Norsea owned, cloaked in colourfully dyed cloth, while two men rowed. One of them was a giant of a man, doing four fifths of the work, his enormous frame entirely obscuring Consada's son, Dalric, from view.

"Welcome, my friend," Elric exclaimed with outstretched arms. Consada only dipped his head slightly to acknowledge Elric's presence; the least possible gesture, without being rude. Maldred however, he ignored completely, still bitter that he had chosen not to visit Norsea the previous day, his offence only slightly mellowed by his knowledge of Lind's death.

"We have much to discuss," Elric said as he led the way to his roundhouse. "Matters of grave concern."

"You speak of these raiders?"

"I do. Stromgalee. A brutal wretch, with many men, and boats," Elric added, keen to get across the seriousness of the matter.

"How do we know it's not just talk?" Consada asked, fixing an inquiring stare upon Maldred as the three men joined Isena by the fire, where a pungent eel broth was bubbling.

"I have seen what he left behind. Burning villages," Maldred said, staring back with contempt. "I travelled some twelve villages. Ten of them told of how they paid him off with some item of value, or other," he explained, at last transferring his gaze to the dancing flames of the fire, as if disturbed by what he knew.

"And the other two villages?" Isena asked after a long pause, as if prompting the punchline to a joke.

Maldred shook his head. "Nothing left, but ash and tears."

"Well I can assure you both that Norsea won't be paying off raiders," Consada declared as he pushed back his long but receding hair from his face. "Even if they do come, they'll probably not cross the lake," he added, glaring at Maldred.

"As two villages, we would have the numbers to see them off," Isena blurted, before Elric could speak.

"Battle? These people are farmers, hunters, craftsmen. There's not a fighting man amongst the lot of them," Consada argued dismissively.

"There wouldn't need to be a battle. We would post lookouts on the river," Elric began, explaining something he had clearly given great thought. "The lookouts would give your people time to cross the lake."

"Cross the lake?" Consada boomed. "Why don't you come and defend Norsea?"

Elric smiled at the foolishness of his statement. "They have to pass Fengate to reach Norsea," he said in amazement, half wondering if the statement was a joke.

"They can ravage Fengate without touching Norsea," Consada roared, as he leapt to his feet, his hands shaking with anger.

"Dalric," he yelled as he stormed across the tiny village, to his log boat. "Put the wretch down, boy, and get back to the boat," he growled at his son, who was fondling the potter's daughter, amongst a pile of thatching reed.

"So, we pay them," Elric said with a sigh, from the hut doorway, as he watched Consada kick a sheep from it's feet and throw a fish trap at a child.

"Ask the seer," Maldred said in a most downbeat and withdrawn manner. "He will know what to do, or if it will happen at all."

Elric looked back at him with pity. He wanted to reason with him, to remind him of the misery the seer's prophesy had brought, but he couldn't find words that wouldn't offend and upset. "You have great faith in the seer?" he eventually asked, after some consideration.

"We might not like what he sees, but there's no doubting he sees it."

Elric sucked his bottom lip and looked at his feet in deep thought. Though not wanting to be seen doubting the seer's value, he so wanted to advise Maldred against listening to the old man.

"I will fetch him," Isena said, with a sudden flourish of energy, hurrying from the roundhouse. "He will surely know if we should worry."

Elric returned to the stew pot and scooped a generous helping for himself and Maldred. "All the more for us, my friend," Elric said, in a respectably drab tone, to match Maldred's mood.

"What will you offer, if he comes?" Maldred asked, accepting the broth graciously, in contrast to his distaste for it, only a day earlier.

"We have two oxen. We'll offer him one, and if that doesn't please him, we'll give up the other," Elric said optimistically. "That should do it."

Maldred didn't respond. Instead he once more fixed his gaze on the flames of the fire. His mind was wandering, preoccupied by matters that troubled him beyond even the death of his son. "Where's your daughter?" he eventually asked. "I've not seen her today."

Elric looked to him with concern. "She spends much of her time chasing sheep out of the marsh." He took a long sup of the broth, before asking the question he had deliberately not asked previously. "What did the villages pay with?"

"Axeheads and spears, those who had them... One village had a master boat builder. They were able to offer a fine boat. They were the fortunate ones." Maldred spoke without taking his eyes off the flames, such was his state of mind.

"And the others?"

"How is the broth, Maldred. I've started adding a new herb," Isena interrupted as she led the seer into the roundhouse.

"Most favourable," Maldred said obligingly, not having taken so much as a sip. He stood as a matter of respect for the seer, as the old man shuffled his way to the fireside, sitting on one of the fur covered logs.

Maldred watched in anticipation as the old man sat beside him, taking the bowl of broth from his hand. He placed it on the floor, by his feet and took from his belt a small leather pouch. His hands were bony and gnarled. They could have easily belonged to a long dead corpse, yet they seemed to function efficiently as he tore up pieces of the fungus, which Maldred had given him the day before, sprinkling them into the broth.

He gazed into the bowl for some time, studying the pattern the floating pieces formed, before eventually raising the bowl to his withered lips.

Elric supped his broth as he impatiently waited for the old man to fall under the potion's spell, causing Isena to scornfully glare at him. He looked out of the entrance, time and time again, frustrated by the fact that the old man was, once more taking a part in the decision making of the village.

The old man put his head in his hands, as if it gave him great pain, eventually rolling on the floor, huddled in a tight ball, dangerously close to the fire. Isena rushed to stop him rolling into the fire, but Elric grabbed her wrist. "The spirits will allow him no harm," he said dryly, as he at last took interest in events, fascinated to see if the old man burned.

More than two minutes passed, before the seer began to regain consciousness. Isena and Maldred helped him to the log, while Elric helped himself to more broth. "I definitely approve of the new herb," he commented lightly, whilst picking a fish bone from between his teeth.

Both Maldred and Isena ignored Elric. They fiercely believed in the power of the seer, and were entirely captivated as he considered speaking.

"What did you see? Will they come?" Isena pleaded as the old man opened his eyes widely.

"Give him time, Woman," Maldred said, in an uncharacteristically disrespectful tone.

"They will come," the old man uttered, his face all but devoid of expression and his mouth partially open, as if he'd had a terrible shock. "There will be choices. Terrible choices, and from it will emerge a great lord... Who that lord will be, depends upon the choices."

Elric at last took an interest. He knew regardless of his beliefs, the seer's words had power in the eyes of others. "What choices do I have to make?" Elric asked, bringing a small smile to Isena's face. The idea of Elric genuinely believing in the seer, brought her comfort.

"When hope is all but lost, a choice will be presented. Upon that choice, much will depend, but the choice will be yours and yours alone." The old man stared deep into his eyes, as he spoke, as if reading his thoughts. "The path you seek is the one into the unknown. A leap into unmeasured waters... Beyond that there is nothing to see, but the shadow of greatness."

"They have him. Hiam, the potter. He has him," Eldwan called from the entrance, amid a flurry of excitement in the village.

Elric and Isena hurried from the roundhouse, assuming Maldred would follow, but he didn't. He stayed, his mind dominated by the thought that had plagued him since Lind's death, a day earlier.

"Can you tell me wise one, will I have more sons?" he asked, his voice filled with desperation. "I'm a wealthy man, I would be able to buy a woman, two even, of breeding years."

The old man took another leather pouch from his belt and from that he drew a pinch of dust. As he had the previous day, he threw it into the fire, and watched the flames. The results weren't as dramatic, the flames altered only slightly but they persisted, absorbing all of the old man's concentration.

"You've seen before, knowledge of the then, will blight the now," the old man said, appealing to him not to ask, as he gripped Maldred's arm with his bony hand.

"I have to know, has my time been for nothing?"

"You have a long path ahead, but weak. So faint that there is almost nothing to it. A half life. A wretched existence, not fully dead, nor fully alive."

Chapter 5

Hiam had become suspicious, having witnessed Andura venture off, into the marshes, with two different people. He had laid in wait, until the three had left Vintnor, to claim his prize. Maldred had offered the prize of two unused axes to the man or woman who found him; a significant step back from his boat and it's contents, which he had been offering the day before, when grief blinded his judgement.

Vintnor limped into the village, with a rope on a slip knot, tied tight around his neck. From time to time Hiam yanked the rope, not for any practical purpose, just because he could, because it made him feel powerful.

The villagers watched as Vintnor struggled with every laboured step, to the Thane's roundhouse; Hiam increasing the pressure on the rope, as if to demonstrate his power over the injured young man.

"Maldred," Elric called. "It is him. Our potter has caught him for you."

Vintnor awaited Maldred's emergence from the roundhouse, knowing there was a good chance he might be killed on the spot. Maldred appeared flustered. He took some seconds to compose himself, before reaching back into the roundhouse doorway for his axe.

Vintnor braced himself, in preparation to meet the spirits. He forced himself to a more upright position, hoping to die with a degree of dignity and pride. Despite the events of the previous day, it seemed so wrong to see Maldred launch himself with a vengeful axe, bent upon his destruction.

Only as the blow was about to be struck, did Elric grudgingly intervene, grabbing Maldred's arm by the elbow. "There are ways to do this properly," Elric insisted. "By ritual, as an offering. It's the only way to see it ends here."

Isena looked on, troubled by what she saw as Elric's weakness. "Let our friend have his revenge," she argued. "He is his property."

"And this is my village. Not his. Not yours," Elric snapped in a quite out of character manner. "You'll have your blood, but at a fitting time, in a fitting manner."

"An offering?" Isena asked in a more mellow tone.

"The spirits of the water might just guide Stromgalee down the river, without troubling us," Elric suggested optimistically.

"This is madness," Vintnor gasped pulling the rope around his throat loose, for long enough to speak. "They were trying to kill me."

"That is their right," Isena hissed back, before Hiam yanked on the rope, hard, to ensure Vintnor did not speak to them again. As he blundered to his knees, Vintnor caught sight of Andura, peering out from behind one of the roundhouses, visibly distressed.

Isena also noticed her. She fixed an accusing stare upon Andura, who in turn looked away in shame, as if to confirm her guilt.

"Tomorrow is the night of the round moon. A sacred time. We'll slaughter some sheep; make a feast of it. An appeal to the spirits for protection," Elric said in the bold manner that made him a natural Thane; a manner that didn't accept arguments. "Lash him to the pole in the mean time. The whole village can guard him, there."

The pole stood alone, near to the centre of the village. On occasion, over the years, people had been tied to it for a day, for trivial offences, but that was as severe as punishments had needed to be, during Elric's time as Thane. It had been a time of peace, but even with every faith in the spirits, few doubted that those times were coming to an end.

Vintnor sat with his back to the pole, while Hiam and Eldwan yanked on lengths of honeysuckle twine, cutting hard into his flesh, tying it again and again, not just to secure him, but to deliberately cause pain. Vintnor didn't speak, or protest. He knew there was nothing he could say to them, that would change their minds.

As he gazed out, across the reed encircled lake, he watched the people of Norsea, gathered, watching him. It seemed strange. He had been all but invisible to the people he met. No more than a tool, or livestock, at best. Now he was the centre of interest. For a moment he allowed himself to enjoy the attention, before his mind was brought back to the then, by a child throwing a handful of pig dug, which splattered his tunic.

He waited for Hiam to leave. He was keen to collect his axes from Maldred, and so, was quick to go. "How do they plan to do it," he asked Eldwan, hoping he might be of a kinder nature than Hiam.

Eldwan rubbed his balding head, considering the question, and how to answer, or even if he should answer. "You are very fortunate," he began, before pausing for further consideration. "You are to be with the spirits of the water. A gift."

"How do you plan to kill me?" Vintnor insisted, in a clear and plain tone.

"There will be some words said. A lot of words. Praises to the spirits of the water... You'll be made to kneel," he said, before pausing. "You must understand that we need the spirits to help us, and Maldred would have killed you anyway."

"Why do you need your spirits. Are you all so shit useless that you can't help yourself," Vintnor barked at him. "How are you bastards going to kill me."

"Your head will be dented with a large rock, and your stomach opened. The rock will be,... It will be, sewn in, to take you down to the deepest part of the lake, where the spirits dwell." Eldwan looked away from him as he stuttered his explanation. "A time of pain, followed by an eternity with the spirits."

"If it's so wonderful, why don't you have a go," Vintnor yelled at him, as he scurried away, causing himself yet more attention. He refocused his vision on the lake, watching as the log-boats returned for the night; some carrying fish and eels, and another, a deer, which had drowned in the river. Even then, with the threat of Stromgalee at their door, he saw their life as enviable.

"Is it right you killed the trader with a spear, from the width of the great river?" the boy asked, who had thrown the pig dung minutes earlier.

"No, it wasn't that far. Just a lucky shot," Vintnor replied with a gentle smile.

"They're saying it was, and they're saying you were swimming at the time. They're saying the sun god was angry at the traders and guided your spear," the boy bubbled with excitement, talking to Vintnor as if he were a great hero.

"They're saying a lot, aren't they," Vintnor joked.

"They are. They're calling you the Truespear."

"Well I'll be the dead spear before long," Vintnor replied, holding back a smirk for the compliment.

"The Sun God won't let you die. You see," the boy said thoughtfully, as he hurried away at the sight of his mother approaching.

Prompted by the boy's words, Vintnor looked to the setting sun. They were words many a man would have gladly bought into, especially when faced with his hopeless position, but Vintnor didn't think like that. He didn't disrespect the gods and spirits, nor did he live his life by them.

The smell of cooking meat was teasing his senses. The steam and smoke from a large cooking fire was blowing across the village, on an increasing breeze. He watched as the birch trees began to sway. "It's going to be close," he muttered to himself as he quietly calculated the course of Stromgalee's raiding party, along the river.

The sight of Andura and Eleena, carrying large bowls of food, from the direction of the cooking fire, raised his spirits further. He studied them, as they approached. Eleena was an enigma; a curiosity to be given deeper thought another day, should another day come, but Andura, she was of great beauty, a picture a man could fix in his head and take happily to his grave.

"I was expecting to be given the bones to suck," he commented at the sight of the hefty feast he was being presented with, centred around an entire leg of lamb.

"It's all for you," Andura said, smiling quite falsely as she struggled to make the best of the situation. "You must be strong for the journey ahead."

Vintnor looked at her enquiringly, assuming she planned to help him escape. "I'm constantly watched," he whispered, half expecting her to cut him free, there and then.

"No, there's nothing we can do to stop that," Eleena replied, as she took a hand full of moss from a bowl of warm water and began to wash him. "You must be well cared for, when you go to the spirits... Fed, washed, loved even. We can't send you to their realm appearing unwanted." As she spoke, she adjusted the ropes around the lower part of his body and slid his legs to a more comfortable position. She looked around, to see at least six people watching, but it did not bother her, it was all part of the preparation to her.

Be it jealousy or embarrassment, Andura placed the food by his side, turned her back and hurried away as Eleena lifted her skirt and straddled him.

Chapter 6

The night had slowly descended into a summer storm. Wind and rain had lashed the village for much of the night, yet still Vintnor was constantly watched.

With the morning sun, the rain of the night before seemed instantly forgotten, for all but him, who was entirely saturated.

"Will the spirits still want me if I die of bloody cold," Vintnor called out to Eldwan, shivering in a huddled ball, and still tightly bound to the pole.

"You had a bit of a warming last night, from how I understand it," Eldwan replied with a lecherous grin. "Different to what she'll be doing to you tonight."

Vintnor considered Eldwan's words carefully, while Eldwan fetched a sheepskin from his house. He had fooled himself that she might be the one to set him free. In reality, her riding him in the moonlight was just the first stage of a deadly ritual.

"Sunshine before the storm?" Vintnor suggested as Eldwan returned with the sheepskin.

"That's about it," he replied. "Be thankful, when my time comes I'll be lucky if they bother digging a hole."

"Eels have got to eat," Vintnor said with an agreeing smile.

"Has the old fool tried to bother you any more?" Eldwan asked as Maldred lurked impatiently, by his boat.

"Can't look the way I am. Silly old bastard knows who got his son killed. He just can't face it." As he spoke, Vintnor's attention was taken by a gathering, across the lake, on the Norsea shore. The high pitched bleating of a sheep could be heard, as the animal was promptly put to death and loaded into a log boat, to be deposited in the depth of the lake. He laughed. "You poor stupid bastards are more scared than I am... At least I got a hump out of the deal."

Eldwan walked off without saying another word. The truth was the sharpest weapon Vintnor had to hand, and it definitely had a sting to it.

After a brief and fruitless tug on the twine, which held him, Vintnor began to look around for Andura.

"You won't see her, boy," came the husky, aged voice of the seer, from behind him. "She is the most valuable thing this village has. A Thane's daughter would be a great prize for the raider lord."

Vintnor lowered his eyes with sorrow, as he considered the price the village would pay. "Then how does the Thane plan to pay them off?"

The old man ignored his question walked around him, putting his head to one side, as if trying to view him from every angle. "Are you the man that talks to spirits?" Vintnor asked, disturbed by the old man's behaviour. Again, the old man did not answer. He took one step back and, without warning, threw a hand full of feathers into Vintnor's face. He held his hand out, silently instructing Vintnor not to move the feathers from where they had landed.

"You won't die today," the old man uttered, deeply distracted by the feathers, as he studied their positions. "You will find a place in a world that does not yet exist... Yours is a path of blood, a path without joy. You will be like the sapling in the winter sun. You will cast the shadow of a mighty tree, but never forget, you will only ever truly be a slave."

Vintnor listened to his words respectfully. He knew the great belief Maldred had in the old man, and therefore took him seriously. "What do I need to do, to gain this great future."

The old man slapped his face, without warning. "Listen boy, bloody well listen... Your path will carry you no more joy than the boat that would drop your slaughtered corpse in the lake."

The slap came as a puzzle to Vintnor. It was delivered with force, greater than he would have believed possible from such a frail old man, but it did not anger him. It's function was to focus his mind entirely, upon the few hours ahead. He considered his situation. He was bound with honeysuckle twine. He still had hidden a sharpened flint, which would make light work of that. He looked at the villagers around him. He was faster and stronger than any one of them.

  He locked eyes with the old man, as if to acknowledge what he had been told, but not another word was spoken between the two. While he was awkwardly twisting his arms around, he asked himself why he had so easily given himself over to the will of Maldred and the villagers. First, he considered some kind of magic or witch craft; perhaps something to do with Eleena, or the spirits themselves. Ultimately the conclusion he came to was more unsettling; it was what he had become, in every way a slave, a subordinate, an obedient servant, who obeyed mindlessly, even in the face of death. As he began to discreetly cut away at the twine, he considered the old man's words further. Was he predicting that he would never change from that path, or that he would simply be someone's oarsman for life. Everything the old man said seemed to be a contradiction, yet for reasons he did not understand, he believed every word.

  At the very second the first of his bindings sprung loose, Vintnor noticed something strange, on the opposite side of the lake. At first it was just a child running. Nothing drastic, just enough to gain his attention. The boy was running at a sprint, and began to shout something inaudible, which in turn seemed to gain the attention of others, on the Norsea shore.

  He listened intently to his surroundings. As Norsea began to panic, Fengate fell silent. People stopped what they were doing, watching the Norsea shore. Even the birds on the lake and in the trees, stopped to assess the threat, considering the merits of flying to safety.

  Vintnor secreted his flint back under his tunic, as the first of Stromgalee's men appeared in Norsea, charging from the reeds.

"They're coming. They're coming," he heard Dugan shout, moments later, as the quite unfit young man came blundering from one of the paths, which led to the river.

Elric seemed to appear instantly from his roundhouse, where he had spent much of the day, discussing the threat of attack. "Carry on about your work. They're visitors, just like any other," Elric announced to his people as they began to run. "Please, stay. We will negotiate," he insisted, grabbing a woman as she ran past him. She wriggled free, terrified, determined to run to the marshes. He looked to the channel, which connected their lake to the river. It remained empty, the water almost undisturbed, but for a duck and her ducklings, swimming casually towards the mooring.

"Bring the oxen. Just one of them," he called to one of Eldwan's sons. "Please, don't panic," he pleaded loudly, in the hope that someone at least might take heed of his instruction.

"I'm not panicking," Vintnor said smugly, as the frightened woman came running back, being pursued by two of Stromgalee's men.

The sound of screaming from both villages, gave Vintnor no joy, but as Elric stood, frozen by fear and helplessness, he couldn't forget that he was the man who planned to have him put to death, in the most horrible way.

As raiders emerged from the birch and reeds, behind the roundhouses, Maldred hurried to his boat, with his axe in his hand. "No my friend, please, no," Elric shouted.

Maldred stood with his back to his boat, facing off two of the raiders. "Are we not guests?" one of the largely leather clad warriors asked, with an imposing grin.

"Not to my boat, you're not," Maldred snarled back, standing square. He was wearing his heavy fur, despite the warmth of the day. In his mind, it gave his the strength of the animal that once wore it. At very least, it helped to hide the frailty of his advancing years.

"What have we here. A warrior?" the booming, arrogant voice of Stromgalee called, from a large boat, as it emerged from the reed lined channel.

"A man protecting what's his, that's all," Maldred growled back as he turned to face him.

Stromgalee leapt from his boat with a massive stride, before he was even close to the mooring, demonstrating his agility and intimidating Maldred in the process. He looked in the bottom of Maldred's boat, evaluating it's contents.

"Yours?" he asked, stepping into the boat. "You're not from here, are you?"

"I'm not... I travel," Maldred replied sternly, brandishing his axe in both hands, effectively demonstrating his lack of combat experience.

"That's what I thought. You see, these people have invited us here. Isn't that right, Thane, or chief?" Stromgalee exclaimed, grinning at Elric, his every action designed to intimidate.

"That's right," Elric agreed with a voice weakened by fear. "We mean you no harm."

"Just you then, trader," Stromgalee laughed as he began to rummage through the bundle of bronze tipped spears, on the deck of Maldred's boat. "How about it then trader, you and me, first cut. If you can open my flesh, even a scratch, I'll let you sail away. I win, I get the boat." Every word, movement and gesture Stromgalee made was for show; for the entertainment of his men, or more accurately to maintain the respect of his men.

"I shouldn't need to fight for something that is already mine," Maldred snapped back. Stromgalee's men laughed and jeered at his words. Their numbers were increasing by the minute, coming in from all directions, droving ahead of them villagers who had tried to run.

"Come on trader, I promise not to kill you. I can't be fairer than that."

Maldred turned and shooed away three of the raiders, who were crowding him. "Give a man some space to fight, will you," he demanded, taking care to show no fear.

Once more Stromgalee grinned broadly, in such an exaggerated manner that it was surely, like everything else about him, just part of an act. He picked up one of Maldred's spears and inspected it, as he stepped out of the boat. He stood in front of Maldred casually, and rubbed the edge of the bronze tip on his arm. "My compliments," he began, as he counted seven hairs from his arm, on the incredibly sharp edge. "An edge a man can be proud of."

"Here's another," Maldred roared, swinging his axe with every bit of strength he had. He paced forwards with the swing, taking the fight to Stromgalee, trapping the raider lord between himself and the water's edge.

Stromgalee was more than twenty years younger that Maldred and agile with it. The cumbersome swing of Maldred's axe carried the force to cut it's victim wide open, but used with such force, it was slow to change course. As Stromgalee took two paces to Maldred's right, the likely-hood of Maldred's blade reaching flesh waned. For just a moment, as his swing had clearly become over reached, Maldred realise the terrible mistake he had made. A moment after that, he felt the smart of Stromgalee's spear on the back of his legs. It wasn't a feeling of cut flesh, as he'd expected. It was a nervous pulse that shot through his body, an agonising pain that instantly dropped him to the floor.

Maldred fell, firstly to his knees, then face down in the mud, the backs of his legs pumping with blood. "You see old man, I told you I would not kill you," Stromgalee gloated, gazing down at his fallen adversary. "Bloody fine metal," he uttered, turning his back on Maldred, with no view to looking back.

Eldwan's son, Evan stood, petrified, holding the oxen, which Elric hoped to offer as payment, to leave the village undamaged.

Only then, as Maldred laid in a puddle of his own blood, the idea of such a band of cut throats, being paid off with a single ploughing beast, seemed unlikely.

"What have we here," Stromgalee boomed, to the cheers of his men. He picked up Maldred's bloodied axe and paced at speed towards Evan and the beast, beginning a vast swing as he approached. At the last second, Evan released his grip on the animal's rope lead, crippled by fear. The axe dug deep into it's thick skull, knocking it from its feet, instantly dead. "We feast," he yelled, holding his blood stained arms out to receive praise.

Those who dared, looked on with shock, as their treasured ploughing animal lay, quivering in the dirt, its eye overly open, casting a haunting stare.

Isena hurried to Maldred, who laid, rolling in the mud, by the water's edge. As the blood so quickly pumped from his body, dirt seemed to react with it and formed a crust. "Lay still. It'll be alright," she insisted, but what she could see was drastic. Both legs had a gaping gash below the knee, laying wide open. She looked back to Elric, to silently share what they both knew; Maldred was crippled.

"Slice it up men," Stromgalee ordered, despite the fact that six of them were already cutting away at the beast, like a pack of wild dogs. It was as if he needed to give the order, to give the impression of control.

"Join me by my fire," Elric said weakly, shocked by the brutality of their actions, and distracted by the screams coming from the Norsea village.

Stromgalee looked Elric in the eyes. He stared deeply for what seemed to Elric, an eternity. "Definitely, later," he eventually replied. "For now I would like to explore your village."

Elric struggled to contain his distraction as the screams went on. His eyes were drawn by the sight of a Norsea woman being ravaged by two raiders. "Do excuse my brother. He is sensitive. Takes very little to offend him. He honoured your neighbours with his visit. They were clearly not as welcoming as your people." Stromgalee had a habit of grinning when he spoke, as if to goad and tease, to push people to the limits of their tolerance.

Elric could not find the words to reply. Instead he turned sharply, grabbing Isena as she charged towards him, with clenched fists. In turn Stromgalee walked away, pretending he hadn't seen anything.

"If we contain ourselves, we might yet get everyone through this alive," Elric whispered as he forced her back towards Maldred. "That's what will happen if we don't." Elric angrily pointed across the lake, to the sight of the first Norsea roundhouse, burning.

"Come on, let's get him inside," Isena said bitterly, knowing Elric was right, but furious with it.

"Hey. Thane. What's this wretch?" Stromgalee barked disrespectfully across the village, as he happened across Vintnor, still tied to the pole.

"A slave, Lord. Nobody of concern," Elric called back, as he and Isena began to drag Maldred's hefty weight back to the hut, the task being made awkward by the wounds to the back of his legs.

"Not such a poor village, to afford slaves," Stromgalee shouted back as he studied Vintnor. He looked him deeply in the eyes, as he estimated his worth. "Why are you tied, boy?"

"They plan to throw my dead carcass in the lake, for the water spirits, so that you don't come, lord," Vintnor said with a smirk.

"Should have been a bit quicker about it, Thane man," Stromgalee boomed, delighted by the idea. "So, What do you say. Do you think you could follow a man such as me, and my young brother, of course."

Vintnor looked across the lake, where the young woman had struggled from her attackers, and was running, naked, into the reeds, only to be run down by another of the raiders. He remained silent for a moment as he refocused his vision to the centre of the lake, where he was to be offered to the spirits.

"Depends if you plan to smash my head in with a rock," Vintnor finally answered, with an agreeable smile, having evaded giving a direct answer.

With a single uninhibited swing of his axe, Stromgalee sliced through the twine, where it met the pole, the blade passing so close to Vintnor's wrists that he felt the wind on his skin. "You'll be a slave no more, but cross me, and I'll skin you. Understand?"

"Understand," Vintnor agreed as he leapt to his feet. He fixed his stare to Maldred's boat. "You'll be needing a boatman for that one," he announced as he unwrapped the last of the twine from his wrists. "Reckon I could sail her with my eyes shut."

"You'll get your chance, boy," Stromgalee laughed, as he carried on across the village, exploring its worth. "Now fill you belly. We sail in the morning."

Vintnor stood, in so many ways alone. The smoke of Norsea burning, began to hang on his lungs. 'Was this to be what he would become?' That question played on his mind as heavy as Eleena's rock would have done. He watched as the raiders hacked away at the oxen, some taking slices to the fires to cook; some eating it raw, just to appear even more animal like than they already were.

He felt a sense of being watched. He looked to the Thane's roundhouse, to see Elric standing in the doorway, studying him, as he had been studying Stromgalee's men. The two made eye contact for a second. What they shared was not the hatred that might be, but a distrust, driven by circumstance.

Chapter 7

It was more than two hours, before Stromgalee returned to the Thane's roundhouse. He had walked amongst the villagers; talked to them, terrifying them, but not physically harmed one of them. As he settled by the fire to negotiate terms with Elric, he felt he knew the village as well as if he lived there himself, and he knew its very limited worth.

He entered Elric's house as if he owned it, sitting by the fire, before he spoke a word. "You keep an untidy house, lady," he said to Isena as he gestured towards Maldred, who was laying, curled up in a ball, by the wall.

"Maldred is our guest, as you are, Lord," Isena replied as she stoked the fire.

Stromgalee replied with a low groan; little more than a disapproving grunt.

Elric was uncomfortable with his presence, and it showed. He sat by the fire, prodding stray twigs back into the flames, considering his words. "We understand it is tradition to offer you gratitude for your visit," Elric began, without raising his vision from the flames.

"Just a single item. It brings a village good luck. Protects them from fire, I'm told... I must be a lucky spirit!" Stromgalee cast his menacing grin as he spoke.

"You've already taken our oxen," Elric said nervously.

"You would surely feed your guests?" Stromgalee replied, as if offended.

"Of course, but you will have noticed we have little to give."

"How about the fire from your hearth?" Stromgalee suggested, with a straight face, knowing the tradition that if the Thane's fire is lost, the village must cease to be. After a few seconds he grinned. "Don't worry," he laughed. "I wouldn't do that to you."

Isena stood in front of him, rigidly and nervous. "We can offer you a Thane's wife... That would surely be a prize." She raised her skirt above the knee, to clarify just what she was offering.

"Is that right, Thane man, are you offering me your wife?"

Elric nodded solemnly, unable to look at either of them.

"Tell me, when you have guests, honoured, respected guests, do you drag a bloated, drowned sheep from the marshes, to feed them?.. Or do you offer up a young tender animal?" Stromgalee spoke with anger for the first time, truly terrifying them both. "Come with me, Thane man, and bring your drowned sheep."

He led them from the roundhouse, out, into the village. The sight he wished them to see was clear and shocking. Norsea was glowing. Every house, but one, had burnt, and was smouldering, as was anything that would burn. Dead livestock were being loaded onto a boat, on the Norsea side, and the smell of burning flesh filled the air.

"My brother honours you with a visit," Stromgalee declared as the silhouette of a smaller boat slowly progressed across the lake. The regular rhythmic splash of a pair of oars seemed to relentlessly highlight it's approach. Only as it came into the light of one of the cooking fires, on the lake shore, did anything more than shadows become visible.

Two men were rowing, and a third sitting. "I smell ox, brother," the sitting man boomed with a voice full of joy.

"This is my brother, Treen," Stromgalee announced. "He's a more sensitive type. Best not offer him, drowned sheep," he whispered, as if offering good advice. "Our hosts were about to tell us of their beautiful daughter!"

Elric looked to Isena nervously, who in turn glared at Stomgalee with hate and loathing.

"Did you think your villagers would let you hide your most valuable asset, while they paid?" Stromgalee laughed.

"Why do you do this?" Isena dared to demand. "How does it help you?"

"Look at my men. Do you see one of them hungry, or one that has to dig or hunt for his food?"

"Or one that's short of a hump," Treen added as he pulled his boat ashore. He was a giant of a man, more than six and a half feet tall and big with it. In contrast to Stromgalee, he was full bearded, with long, untied hair, hanging down his back. As he stepped closer, gazing down at Elric, he came into sharp focus, in the firelight. His brown beard and face were smothered in blood; more blood than would have found its way there naturally.

He stared Elric in the eyes, quite deliberately to intimidate. Only after many terrifying seconds, did a broad smile stretch across his stone cold face. "I nearly forgot. A gift for the bride's parents."

Treen turned and reached back into the dark of the boat, picking through the spear shafts. "Nobody needs a neighbour like that," he announced in such a light manner that you could have expecting he was offering a bunch of flowers, rather than the head of Consada, impaled on a spear.

"He smiles now," Treen laughed, bedding the spear shaft into the ground to display his prize, before pushing the corners Consada's mouth upwards.

Isena turned to run back to the roundhouse, only to be grabbed by the arm, by Stromgalee. "Know this, drowned sheep. My men have gone to collect our bride, and they have a guide. They won't come back empty handed."

"The slave?" Elric asked, as Isena wriggled free and ran to the roundhouse.

Stromgalee grinned. "Like I said, not everyone's prepared to suffer for you keeping what's yours safe."

Elric once more looked across to Norsea. "Why have you left the Thanes roundhouse unfired?"

"You know why," Treen replied, before striding away to join the other raiders.

He knew then that the fire in the Thane's house had been extinguished; the most powerful curse that could be bestowed upon a village. His vision was drawn to the head of Consada; a man he had never liked, yet now his mutilated head represented the end of the life they had all once known. "How will my daughter be treated?" he asked, with a defeated tone.

"Like a queen," Stromgalee grinned, as he revealed in Elric's misery.

Vintnor had been watching from the shadows. He couldn't hear what was said, but Consada's head on a spike and Isena's hurried, upset exit, spoke many words.

His mind was engulfed by the scene before him; the life he must lead, to live at all. He remembered his family, and the life they had; not so different to the life of the villagers, until hunger came.

"Mean bastards, aren't they," the youthful voice of a boy of about thirteen commented from behind him. He'd stopped to rest, from dragged a very large dead pig, towards a moored boat. He Carried a club on his belt, not yet being trusted to wield a weapon of value, but the boy was every bit a raider, in all that he did.

"I thought Stromgalee only expected one gift," Vintnor asked. "These people will struggle to see the winter through."

"That was before they tried to hide the Thane's daughter," the boy bubbled, excited by the prospect of yet more pillage. "Anyway, I thought you would be glad to see them starve... Weren't they going to do you in?"

"They're no concern of mine," Vintnor said harshly. "Just keen to know if your leader's word is to be trusted, if I'm to serve him."

"You really are a bloody slave, aren't you... You can start serving your new master by helping me with this bloody swine." The lad spoke with cheek and mischief. He clearly had freedom within Stromgalee's camp, maybe even respect.

"Is one of them your father?" Vintnor asked, gesturing towards a group of Stromgalee's men.

"No," the boy replied as he began to drag the pig. "Are you going to bloody help, or not?"

Vintnor was relieved to be helping the boy. It was rapidly becoming his greatest fear that he might be asked to do something his conscience couldn't accept. It was a fear greater than even his impending slaughter, only a few hours earlier; an irony he was fully aware of.

The pig dragged easily with two of them, but the task of loading it into the smallest of Stromgalee's boats, was more challenging, and took several minutes of near silent struggle.

"I'm Vintnor, should you wish to call me something other than slave," he announced as they both sat, to catch their breath, once the pig was safely deposited in the bottom of the boat.

"Balmoor," the lad replied, before pausing to think. "Hard to believe when you look at me, isn't it. I was like the lady they hunt for. The most valuable prize in the village; the Thane's eldest son."

"They sold you?"

"Bargained me away. My father had another son. Saved the village, so I suppose he did right," the boy explained, his voice vague as he considered it.

"But why. What does Stromgalee gain from it?"

"Power… To take a Thane's son as a slave, makes him more powerful than the Thane." The boy spoke as if Vintnor was foolish for not understanding.

"Do they treat you well?" Vintnor asked, being both worried for the boy and his own future welfare.

"I've no complaints. Bloody hell, the food is better," he smiled, but there was an air of sadness in his voice as he considered his past life.

"Well that's us then, a pair of rotten slaves," Vintnor said merrily, to lighten the mood, and bring an end to the boy's story, which was uncomfortably similar to his own.

Chapter 8

Over the course of the night, laughing, chanting and jeering had slowly dwindled as the raiders gradually gave in to their overly full stomachs. Some made up rough beds, amongst the reed piles and animal feed, while others slept in their boats. Just a few; the worst of them, invited themselves into roundhouses.

By morning, the quiet from the Norsea shore was unnatural, and chilling. Many had run, that much the villagers knew. They also knew there had been killings. They'd heard the screams, they'd smelt burning flesh, but nobody knew the extent of the slaughter, or how many had got away, and with the lake effectively off limits, due to Stromgalee's boats, Norsea had to wait.

Elric and Isena were in an impossible position. If Andura was to be captured they would have no choice but to hand her over. Anything suggesting options was simply an illusion, cultured by Stromgalee, for his own vanity. A thin vale to hide his true status of raider lord.

They waited anxiously, never straying more than a few feet beyond the roundhouse entrance. Stromgalee had made it clear to them that if she wasn't found, Fengate would suffer the same fate as Norsea, yet still, deep in their parental hearts, they longed for Stromgalee's men to return empty handed.

It was two hours after dawn, before Stromgalee's men began to gather at the Thane's roundhouse, some of them still high on the brightly coloured fungi, taken from Maldred's boat. "You're in luck, Thane man. They were well hid, but our man Ruke, he can sniff out a woman, even in pit like this." As Stromgalee spoke, a hustle of raiders came into view, at first entirely obscuring them, such was their excitement.

"Take your dirty hands off my woman," Stromgalee boomed, angered as he realised Andura was being manhandled. Only then did the raiders make space around the two women.

"Come now brother, riches are for sharing," Treen joked, immediately calming Stromgalee's rage.

"But the chief gets first pickings," Stromgalee grinned, horrifying Elric and Isena. Elric put his hands to his face in despair. He realised then that even if Stromgalee wanted to keep Andura for himself, he wasn't in control of his men enough to do so.

"Cheer up, Thane man, it's your daughter's wedding day," Stromgalee grinned, before changing his very false tone to one of concern. "You do want me to marry your daughter, don't you?.. You do still give her freely?"

Elric looked at the two young women as they stood, dirty and bedraggled; the sorriest of sights. "Why do you have to do this. Is the other girl not good enough for you," Isena blurted.

"Quiet, drowned sheep," Treen snapped. "Less you want to join our happy friend here." As he spoke he produced the spear, with Consada's head impaled upon it and waved it in her face. Defiantly she refused to turn away, instead choosing to look Consada in the face, preferring that grim sight to the men that stood before her.

"Thane man, I don't believe you've been taking proper care of your wife. I think she's wanting proper men," Stromgalee spoke loudly, encouraging the cheers of his men. "My men are not as choosy as I." His men cheered and shouted, excited by the prospect of being gifted the quite attractive Thane's wife.

Maldred had kept from sight, in the shadows of Elric's roundhouse. He had listened and watched as events unfolded, entirely torn as to what, if anything he should do. His desire for revenge against Vintnor was all that prevented him from proposing what he saw as the solution to Elric's apparently impossible situation.

In contrast to Elric, Maldred's belief in the gods and spirits was strong, to the extent that he considered almost every event to be governed by them. It was only as Isena was directly threatened by the raiders, that he considered he must act.

Ruke stepped forwards, loosening the leather cord, which held his tunic tight. Like Stromgalee he played for the crowd, grinning and prancing as he reached towards her. Her reactions were sharp. She appeared to slap his hand away, but Ruke clutched his wrist from the intensity of the pain. Blood began to drip from between his fingers, first slowly, then faster, from the slash wound, which had cut an artery.

A sharpened fresh water muscle shell laid, smeared in blood, in the dirt. Stromgalee boomed with laughter. "A drowned sheep's done for you, with what great weapon? The remains of her breakfast."

Ruke swung at her with his back hand, sending her flying backwards. He then reached for the nearest villager, and in one brutal motion, tore a section of cloth from the woman's sleeve, before binding his wrist with it. He stepped forwards, deliberately crushing the shell under his leather bound foot.

It wasn't as difficult for Elric to contain his anger as it should have been. He had led his village in a time of peace, and had never known violence. His instinct was to negotiate, but he had nothing to negotiate with.

Maldred was the most pathetic of sights. Dragging himself along on his hands, with his bound legs dragging along behind, like a snake. "It's our trader friend," Stromgalee jeered, as Maldred approached Elric.

Maldred ignored him entirely, focusing all his strength on pulling himself up from the ground, on a large section of tree trunk. Elric was glad of even a moment's distraction. "What is it, my friend?" he asked, concerned that Maldred would be further harmed.

"The seer's prophacy," Maldred insisted. "Hope is all but lost, as he said it would be. You must make your choices. Now is the time."

Elric looked Stromgalee in the eyes, his mind absorbed by what Maldred was telling him. He looked back to Maldred, who was in turn, staring at Vintnor. "Combat," he said loudly to the shock of the onlooking villagers. "I, as Thane of this village, claim the right to choose a champion, to defend the village and my daughter."

Stromgalee grinned with delight, and turned to his men. "Do you here that, Thane man wants to fight," he laughed. "I think his wife is going to fight for him, or perhaps the girl."

Dugan stepped forwards. "I would fight, for you Andura," he said quietly and shyly, like a nervous child.

Andura shook her head and silently mouthed no to him. The cackle of the raiders, intensified with the ever increasing prospect of entertainment. Before another word was spoken, Treen stepped forwards with two spears, handing one towards an ever more confused Dugan.

"That is not my choice," Elric said loudly, with the boldness that such a massive gamble required. "I choose Vintnor the slave, to fight for the village. To fight for my daughter."

Stromgalee stopped laughing, but smiled slightly. "You seem to be confused. You are supposed to choose someone from your side. One of the pigs perhaps," he joked, but still without the laughter.

"He didn't come here with you. He was here already, with us."

"Waiting to be killed!"

"That may be, he was still here."

Stromgalee looked back at Vintnor, who stood baffled by the notion. "What do you say, boy. Will you fight for this pig shit village and the Thane that wanted to smash your head in with a rock."

Vintnor took a deliberate step forwards, to be sure his words were heard. "I will not," he exclaimed clearly and loudly for all to hear. "I will fight for the woman who found me in the marshes and tended my wounds." As he spoke, he looked to Andura with affection, sufficient for any onlooker to understand his motives.

"Then it's settled, Thane man," he said as he focused his attention on Elric. "If the boy wins, we'll leave, but know this, if the boy falls, and he will fall, we'll take everything else."

Elric attempted to look defiant, but he was afraid, and it showed. He looked around. The raiders were joyful, eager for what they saw as entertainment, as they might watch the hawk play with a sparrow, before dispatching it.

Stromgalee began to clear the open area for the contest, shooing the men back like herding livestock. As he did so, Hiam stepped forwards, mumbling something, too quietly for onlookers to hear. Stromgalee looked round and grinned. "Today we fight with axes," he said with delight. "It seems our Thane friend here, is truly a tactical master... The spirits gave him a gift to protect them from, us, and in his great wisdom, Thane man decided to smash his head in as a gift to the spirits... And, if that wasn't enough wisdom, our young friend here, known as the True Spear, when given his freedom, from the said Thane man, chooses to fight those who freed him, for a bit of fanny." Stromgalee laughed loudly with his men, the notion of Treen loosing the fight was beyond their imagination.

Elric glared across the open ground at Hiam, who seemed to shrink back into the gathering of raiders, as a snake might blend into the grass.

"Until the death... Until you kill him, brother," Stromgalee said, in a more serious tone, throwing two axes into the centre of the clearing.

Vintnor pounced at the axes, but he was still weak on his injured leg, slowing his speed and agility. Treen was a giant of a man, being able to barge Vintnor away before he could lay a finger on his axe. Treen swung again and again, always putting himself between Vintnor and his axe. The raiders jeered as victory appeared no more than a formality.

With so many disadvantages, Vintnor attempted to clear his mind. He took three clear paces back and dropped to one knee, staring, studying every movement of his massive opponent. Treen was glad of the time to revel in his own greatness. "The boy begs," he declared, holding his axe high in the air, to court praise. But Vintnor was not begging, he was thinking. He stepped forwards, prompting Treen to take a vast, and hugely powerful swing, at head height. It could have gone either way, but Vintnor managed to find the speed and flexibility to step back from the blade, before stamping his left foot into Treen's kneecap.

The pain seemed to add to Treen's vast strength. As an instinct, he swung his axe arm back, propelling Vintnor, towards his own axe. What followed, happened quicker than any man present could entirely follow. As Vintnor slid past his axe, he first grabbed it, then threw it, all in a matter of little more than a second. Because Treen didn't immediately fall, it took seconds more for the raiders to fully grasp what had happened, despite the axe wedged in the side of Treen's face.

A deadly silence fell, only broken by the rabid roar of Stromgalee, as Treen fell, horrifically dead, to the floor. He launched himself forwards, not at Vintnor, but at Elric, overcome with rage, shock and grief; a concoction of emotion that could have seen the village massacred, there and then. He snatched a spear from the hands of the nearest man. It took all the restraint he could muster to resist forcing the spearhead up, into Elric's skull. As it was, he pushed it so hard into his chin that blood began to trickle down the spear-shaft.

His men seemed to collectively hold their breath as he contemplated killing Elric. The retribution of the spirits for a broken pact was something that terrified them, more even than the grieving rage of Stromgalee. His murderous glare seemed to weaken Elric to the point that he shrunk to his knees, before him.

Ruke's intervention undoubtedly saved Elric's life. Of all the raiders, he was the only one that dared do any more than hold his breath. "The Spirits Lord. A pact was made."

Stromgalee cast his glare back at him, enraged by the interference. He was so unstable now. He could have killed any man or woman present, on either side, such was his blind rage. "My brother has lived much of his life on water. Not a shit infested puddle like this. Proper, open water. That is where he will be rested," he snarled and hissed, only grudgingly lowering the spear, before striking Elric to the ground with its shaft. "When my brother is sailing the eternal sea, I will return, to kill you all, slowly, and miserably." As he spoke, his eyes flitted around, picking out villagers, as if he were trying to physically frighten them to death.

He eventually turned sharply, thundering towards the moored boats, but still entirely ignoring Vintnor's presence. The spear, still in his hand, seemed to frustrate him further, as if it were actually burning him, for the fact that he had not yet killed anyone for his brother's death.

Eldwan's son, Evan; still more of a boy than a man, appeared in front of them, chasing a stray piglet. He considered himself out of harm's way, as his father had instructed, but he could not have imagined just what was going through Stromgalee's mind. He nodded and bowed at the sight of the mourning raiders as they charged to their boats, with Treen's body, stretched out over a fencing hurdle, being carried by six men, such was his vast frame.

Evan didn't see Stromgalee bring his spear to a throwing position, even if he had, all he would have gained was the horror of impending death. Powered by an insatiable rage, the spear entered Evan's ribcage, on his left side, its tip exiting by about three inches, on the right side of his chest. "A taste of what you're all going to get, you bastards," he yelled as the boy laid, quivering on the floor, his screaming mother being wrestled back, in fear of her suffering a similar fate.

Stromgalee was already on his boat, by the time Eldwan caught sight of his dead son. "Hold him," Elric ordered sternly to anyone of a mind to wrestle with the remarkably strong carpenter. Blood was still running down Elric's neck as he approached Eldwan. "Today's not the day, my friend," he said, with a heart of sorrow. "You have two more sons to keep from harm."

Elric looked around him. People were screaming and crying. Not just the women and children. The deepest possible misery had descended upon their village, and it all seemed to be focused upon the dead boy's corpse, like a grim premonition for the fate of every soul present.

To add insult to their collective despair, one of their own stood, on the boat, in the shadow of Stromgalee. Hiam dared to look back on those he had lived his life with; his own family even. He could not answer when his wife screamed the only possible Question; 'Why?'

Whatever he could see through his eyes, the people of Fengate could only see the most loathsome betrayal.

Chapter 9

The villagers gathered nervously, in the hours that followed the death of Treen and Evan, son of Eldwan. Much was said, but nothing of substance. Elric said whatever he needed to calm the panic. He had people gathering weapons and tools; anything that could be used as a weapon, but he knew to fight on their own was certain death.

The event upon which it all depended, didn't take place until early afternoon. Just two people in a single log boat, set off from the Norsea shore. Elric had instructed Eleena to ceremonially wrap Consada's head, with all the ritual honours expected, not of a simple village Thane, but of a tribal chief.

He and Isena, stood at the mooring, with the wrapped head, presented on a polished wooden platter. As Dalric, rowed his mother, Idenica, towards their shore, Isena quietly lectured Elric on the importance of being polite, and just how much they needed the survivors of the Norsea attack. She knew how much Elric hated Consada, still half expecting him to kick the head into the water, for the eels.

"Greetings, friends," Elric announced boldly and ever so slightly too cheerfully, despite their own loss.

Dalric rowed the log boat erratically, never having needed to row anywhere before, such was the spoilt nature of his upbringing. "We have suffered greatly," he announced, stepping awkwardly onto the mooring, while his mother snivelled at the end of the boat, upon the sight of Consada's head.

"There is much to come, I fear," Isena said abruptly, taking the conversation straight to the only point that mattered. "Unless our two villages can unite to to defend ourselves."

Dalric ignored her, focusing entirely upon the bound head. "At least the brutes left us something to present to the spirits," he said, passing the head back to his mother, who cuddled it, like a child with a cherished toy.

"We must talk now, for the good of both our villages," Isena insisted, sensing that Dalric was simply planning to row back to Norsea, with his father's head.

"Not a village any more," Dalric replied, avoiding eye contact. "The Thane's sacred fire was put out. They stood in a circle and pissed on it... Sons of whores."

"And our man killed their leader's brother," Elric added. "They can be killed. We have a man that can kill them."

"We can all kill them, if we arm ourselves and stand together," Isena insisted, almost shouting at Dalric, from frustration.

"Our people are already gathering what little they have left, to leave. It's not a village any more," Dalric explained, dejectedly.

"Then become part of ours," Elric blurted. It was a day dream of his, from time to time. Something he knew was impossible, while the two villagers were thriving, but with Consada gone and both villages facing oblivion, his plan held weight. "Come. I'll show you what I'm talking about."

Elric led Dalric along the bank, to a point, which he knew to be both comparatively narrow, and clear of the movement of boats and fishing. "A path, a bridge, call it what you will. Our two villages would be one. Our woodworkers and fishing, and your fertile cropland. We would be the strongest of villages." Elric spoke with excitement, his arms waving about as he frantically tried to put a picture in Dalric's head.

"I can't be thinking about this now," Dalric complained, turning to return to his log boat.

"But we must think on it," Idenica interrupted, halting his departure. She stood behind him, far more composed than before, but still holding the bloodied cloth bag, containing her late husband's head. "Who would be Thane of this truly great village?" She asked, stepping beside her son, to take over negotiations.

"I would, for now, but I am in the later years of my life, and young Dalric has still much to learn. If he were to marry my daughter, as we have talked of in the past, the succession would be natural. It would be as if he were my heir."

"I am quite able, I assure you," Dalric complained, to which they both entirely ignored him.

Idenica nodded with approval. "You speak as if it were a great chiefdom? Not two ravaged villages."

"Look at where we are placed. Together we could become a trading port, yes, even a chiefdom, in our grand-children's day perhaps."

"You forget the reason we are here. The beasts that did this, come back for you and yours," She held up Consada's head to prove her point. "For this great future you would have the battered and beaten people of Norsea stand beside you and die at the hands of those beasts."

"I would," Elric said, as if it weren't a big thing.

"Our homes have been destroyed, our women degraded. Why would we want to fight?" Idenica demanded, not dismissively, but as if she was looking for a worthy reason.

"Anger," Isena exclaimed. "Rage, revenge. A chance to put matters right." She gestured towards Norsea, to the people pathetically picking through the remains of the burnt roundhouses. "We both know if they leave now, all they'll have is starvation, or cold, should they survive until winter."

Idenica watched for a minute, her mind still open to suggestion and by no means made up. Eventually, with her vision still fixed upon the Norsea shore, she asked, "do you really think you can fight them?"

"The very fact they don't, makes it possible," Elric assured her, loudly for the dozen or so villagers to hear, who had gathered nearby. "The spirits have prepared us for this," he added, knowing that the spirits held greater weight than he did. "Some of you heard it yourselves, from the lips of our enemy. Stromgalee himself admitted it, the spirits sent the True Spear here, so we could be great." Elric was now doing what he did best; talking. He was speaking loudly for the gathering villagers to hear. "We will build a great trackway across the water, to link the fertile lands and the people of Norsea, with Fengate. From such a position we would command access to the river and be strong enough to defend such a chiefdom of wealth."

Unlike the other villagers, the seer did not stand back, to listen. He approached, moving faster than his usual feeble pace, giving Elric cause for concern. He eventually stopped on the very edge of the water, on a grassy tussock, to gain a little height, that his bent form had lost, so he too could be easily heard. By now almost every villager was present, but until the seer had spoken, nothing more Elric could say, would be heard.

"A marriage between the villages would bring prosperity," the old man eventually announced to the enthralled villagers. "I have looked into the smoke and I can see a victory of kinds, for some, at least." The old man stepped down from his tussock and picked a twig from the ground. "The cost of this prosperity is something you should understand." He scraped a crude circle in a patch of bare earth, to represent the lake. He then drew a line across it. "A spear through the heart of the water spirits," he exclaimed, stabbing angrily at the centre of the circle.

As Elric opened his mouth to argue with the seer, Isena rushed to the old man's side. "Then guide us. You said we could succeed, how can this be made to work?" She clutched at the old man's withered arm, begging for his help.

He looked her in the eyes, as he would gaze into a flame or a puddle of sacrificed blood, in search of answers. He looked at her in amazement, as if he had made a great discovery. Once more he turned to his rough drawing, in the dirt and with his twig, he began to draw a circle, half way across Elric's planned bridge.

"This is for man," he explained, pointing to the line which represented the bridge. "And this for the spirits."

Etched into the earth, it didn't look so spectacular, but Elric felt the power the old man carried amongst his people. He had, with a few words and a drawing in the dirt, taken his plans to destruction and back, and added many months of work in the process.

"That can be done," Elric agreed, knowing he had no other choice. "For now, we must prepare."

The old man stared at him, before prodding him with his twig. "That is not the end of it. Not for such an offence to the spirits to be forgiven."

Isena lost every bit of colour from her cheeks. Maybe she had shared the seer's vision, or just sensed the price he was to ask. "Then tell us, redeem us in the eyes of the spirits."

"A gift, you have already refused to another," the old man said bluntly, staring Elric in the eyes as he spoke. "You have time to think. Your offering would not be required until the last timber is laid."

Elric glared at the old man with a hatred, which surpassed his usual dislike and frustration for the old man's regular interference. He thought for a time, considering his response, which would be pivotal to all that followed. "Very well. The spirits must be appeased," he agreed, his tone mellowing as he considered the many benefits of not actually completing the ceremonial section of the causeway.

Isena knew Elric's disrespect for all matters spiritual, well enough to accept his decision with no more than a worried hiss, while the seer took his words at face value, his insight into the there and then being far less clear.

Vintnor knew of the gathering, and he knew his future, if he had one, depended upon it, but he chose not to attend. He sat in the reeds, on the opposite side of the village, deliberately avoiding the discussion.

He was accompanied by Dugan, who had been assigned the task of watching over him, by Elric. Conversation was sparse. Dugan was not a great talker, not of sense, at least. "What's she doing," Vintnor asked, at the sight of Eleena, walking into the reeds, in a white ceremonial gown.

"She's busy. Best not bother her," Dugan said, in a cautionary tone. "Matters of the spirits."

Vintnor immediately jumped to his feet, driven by both curiosity and boredom. "It would be as well if you stay here, then," he said with a wry grin. "Wouldn't want you getting cursed."

Dugan stood, but did not move. He was confused, and gravely worried, in fear of disturbing Eleena's appeals to the spirits, yet, to leave Vintnor unguarded would be to disobey Elric's order. His decision was to stand and stare into the reeds, where Vintnor had vanished from sight.

"Good to know you don't hump everything you plan to sacrifice," he said, by means of announcing his presence.

She turned, not startled or surprised by his being there, but quite ready to talk. Vintnor however, was startled. He had seen the mole in her left hand, and had guessed it to be some kind of sacrifice to the water spirits. He had not expected to see her drenched in its blood. In her right hand she still held the small, deadly sharp dagger, which she had used to bleed the animal. Her white, sparse dress was now bloodied, her breasts barely covered by it, instead obscured by the blood; her legs even blood splattered. "Come, it will protect you in the battle to come." She beckoned him with the knife, as if appealing to the lamb that it was time for slaughter, yet he did not think twice about stepping forwards, ankle deep, in marsh water.

With a forceful hand, she pulled open his tunic and rubbed her bloodied breasts on his chest, before squeezing the already drained mole carcass over his head. "Nothing kills the mole. Nothing will kill you," she explained, mixing the blood with drops of water, to make it go further. "Now be gone. You have much to do before the battle," she said in such a practical tone, as to demonstrate that there was nothing remotely sexual about the intimate ritual.

"I told you not to bother her," Dugan said, at the sight of the blood.

"It was interesting!" Vintnor replied, wiping the blood away with a handful of wet moss. "Now, shall we go and see the other fine maiden of this festering village. I know you're up for a visit with her," he said, with a lecherous smirk.

"What do you want with Andura?"

"Wound dressing," he replied, after a pause to think of an excuse.

Dugan grudgingly nodded. Without speaking, he began to lead Vintnor through the marshes, to a lightly wooded area of dryer ground. As was the rather vague way of Dugan, he just stood amongst the group of about ten large oak trees, as if awaiting instructions.

"Well, where is she?" Vintnor asked impatiently.

Dugan looked behind him, not once but twice, to be sure they weren't followed. "You won't tell?"

"On all that is sacred," Vintnor assured him.

At last Dugan grinned, before pointing to the upstanding roots of a long fallen tree, on the very edge of the reeds. Vintnor studied the area. There was absolutely nothing to see; a few small gorse bushes, on an otherwise undisturbed piece of ground. It was only as he thought about it, that he realised there should be a hole in the ground, where the tree had been upturned.

Tentatively, Vintnor stepped forwards, studying the ground with every step. He pressed the leaf carpeted ground with his toe, expecting it to wobble, yet it remained still. He looked back to Dugan, in the hope of a further clue, but Dugan just looked back with delight that he knew something Vintnor didn't.

Suddenly Vintnor jumped back, as a single sharpened spear appeared from the ground, shortly followed by a woman's giggle.

Dugan laughed hysterically as Andura opened a hatch, at the base of the tree root. "The second mole I've seen today," Vintnor laughed, as she emerged with leaves and cobwebs in her hair.

"It's for the children," she explained as he dropped to his knees and peered inside. What he saw was close to darkness, but he could just make out a selection of pottery storage jars, stacked at the far end, storing food.

"Does the potter know about this place?" he asked with concern.

"Not really," she replied vaguely. "It's just somewhere I came when I was little. I've just fixed it up."

"You should stay with them. Protect the children if they lose."

"You'll be staying?" She asked, while Dugan stood, suddenly rigid, as he remembered his instruction to guard Vintnor.

"I don't know. Nobody has asked me yet. Depends if they want me to fight or if they plan to dam the lake with my corpse!"

"I'm sure there's no talk of that any more. You'll find my father is a lot less bothered by all of that than most. He just has to keep people happy, that's all." While she spoke, she lifted his tunic to view the spear cut on his back. "That looks good, and you've lost your limp. You heal well."

"I have good healers," he replied.

She rubbed a splash of the drying blood from his ear. "I see you've been for more healing?"

"I'm from far away. I don't understand your rituals."

"You understood one of them, from what I saw," she said sharply.

"I was tied, and waiting to have my head smashed in. What did you want me to do?"

"I really don't care," she replied, lost for a more rational answer.

Vintnor jumped into the hole, for a closer look, and to evade further questioning from Andura. "This can go to start with," he muttered, throwing the wood tipped spear from the hole. "Even if they are standing right on top, you won't do anything with that, but get yourself killed."

"I won't be there. It's just for the children."

"You're fighting?"

"My mother was born to a very different people. They fought off raiders many times. Their women were some of the best warriors." Andura spoke of her mother with pride and admiration, but she also spoke with fear. "Anyway, it's my father trying to protect me that's brought this about. I must stand with them."

"Women are for farming and cooking. Not fighting."

"So are slaves," she hissed back at him, before turning her back and stomping off, towards the village. "Come on Dugan. Bring your slave."

Elric was organising the people of both villages, in the area around his roundhouse, as was the tradition to defend the centre of the village, most specifically the Thane's house. Bows, arrows and spears were leaning against the outside walls, and axes dug in the ground for ease of access. Even hand tools and rocks were placed for battle.

Vintnor inspected the few worthy weapons, while Elric watched him with caution. For two or three minutes he walked the perimeter of the roundhouse, dismayed by what he saw. "You should have handed your daughter over," he eventually exclaimed, to deliberately provoke Elric. "She's only going to die, here, with the rest of you."

"Why would you say that?" Elric demanded, clutching a knife, with a broken tip.

"They will surround you. Soften your will and shorten your numbers with arrows, then finish you off with spears, without spilling a drop of their own blood. Your heads will decorate their boats." Vintnor touched the tip of one of the only worthwhile spears, as he spoke, as if to intimidate.

"Your opinion isn't required, only your spear," Elric stepped forwards to demonstrate no fear to the onlookers. "You can stand and fight with us, or you can take a message to the spirits."

"I'm not of a mind to do either, no more than these people are going to be, unless you can offer them some hope of victory."

"What are you suggesting?" he asked with anger. "We're your masters now."

"This is your master." Vintnor touched the tip of the spear again, to further demonstrate Elric's vulnerability. "Fight them in the marshes. Then you'd have a chance. Not much of a chance, but it would be hope for these people to stand."

"We stand in defence of the Thane's fire, as our forefathers did... Tie the filthy slave," Elric yelled, in expectation that all present would seize him.

Both Eldwan and Dugan stood, confused by the speed in which the situation was escalating, and unnerved by the fact that Vintnor was holding one of the few good spears.

Vintnor ignored Elric's words entirely. With the shaft of his spear he etched a circle in the dirt, to represent Elric's roundhouse. "They already know how you are going to fight, because that's how your people always fight, scared shitless of the spirits cursing your village, even if you all get your throats cut... They'll send close to half their number in through the channel, probably led by Stromgalee. The rest will moor a way up river and come across the marshes, as they did before."

Elric was enraged. He considered his words out of hand and above his station, but before he could repeat his order, for Vintnor to be bound, Isena stepped forwards. "Our young friend has a point," she announced to Elric's frustration. "Carry on with you drawing."

"Thank you my lady," Vintnor replied, before etching a crude arrow to represent the raiders attacking across the marshes. "So if we wait in the village, we know we would face them all at once, and we'd be surrounded, we would be killed or enslaved."

"You are already enslaved, boy," Elric snarled.

"Husband, this is how we fought raiders, in the Northern villages." Isena spoke of her tribal upbringing, before her marriage was arranged to Elric. To Elric's annoyance, her words carried weight. She was a Alluni; a renowned warrior tribe and on such matters, the villagers listened.

"We don't have the numbers to send people into the marshes. We need them here, defending the village; the sacred fire." As Elric spoke, he gestured across the lake, to the thane's house, in Norsea, now standing alone, surrounded by only burnt remains of the village that once stood.

"You are not fighters, none of you, but you are marsh men and marsh women. Turn it to your advantage. If you can hide, when they can be seen. If you can move, when they flounder, you will overcome them." Vintnor was now speaking to the people, and they were listening, something that pained Elric, greatly.

"How many would you need?" Elric asked sceptically.

"All of you, every one. Move fast and show no mercy. By the time Stromgalee knows what's happened, half his men will be dead."

"Impossible. The Thane's fire can't be lost... We stand here, and fight for all that's dear... Bind the slave and have no more of this." Elric was defensive. His authority was being over ruled, not only by his wife, but also by someone he considered to be so much below himself.

"What if I were able to defend the Thane's sacred fire?" Eleena interrupted, standing with her grandfather, conspicuously behind her, adding weight to her words. "Then we could all fight in the marshes, to claim the victory the spirits promise us."

Elric stood, belittled, the approving groans and mutterings of the gathered people, confirming their belief in everyone's words, but his. He stood, silently absorbing the scene around himself.

The people of Norsea had lost more or less everything, yet they stood with hope in their hearts, where despair could so easily have taken hold. Eldwan stood with his wife, consumed by a deep sorrow, which left a visible scar on their faces, yet they sought, not just revenge, but a future for their remaining two sons. Even Maldred, laying partially outstretched, like a snake, only propped up on his fists, which Isena had bound in cloth, to stop his knuckles bleeding. These were damaged people, but they weren't broken.

"Very well," he agreed, engulfed by a sense of overpowering weakness. "We will set upon them in the marshes," he announced, as if it were at least partially his idea. "But the slave, known as Vintnor will remain bound until Stromgalee is upon us... He speaks beyond his station."

"What is the reason for this," Vintnor protested as Dugan approached with a length of strong twine.

"You are property. You sold your freedom. Don't expect it back." Elric spoke harshly, embittered by the attitudes of his people and the ease with which Vintnor turned their mood to his requirements.

Andura looked on, with shock. Her father's attitude towards Vintnor was similar to hers, only minutes earlier, yet it seemed so wrong. "Father," she uttered, hoping her presence might mellow his anger, but she could see his mind was set.

Vintnor held his hands together for Dugan to tie, his expression no longer enraged or wronged. He was smiling as Dugan attempted to put the first loop around his wrist, with the spear still held firmly in his hand. "Is that in your way?" he asked obligingly as Dugan fumbled with the twine. "Would you like me to put it some where?.. Up you oversized arse, perhaps," he suggested, still with a good humoured smile, but as he spoke he swung the butt end behind Dugan's legs and, with considerable force, jammed it into the back of his leg, causing him to blunder forwards. Without so much as a breath, he reached forwards, pointing the tip of the spear to Eldwan's throat.

"Your axe," he demanded, his tone suddenly more serious.

Eldwan slid the axe from his belt, slowly passing it to Vintnor, handle first. "It sounds like you are all of a mind to fight for your freedom. Why shouldn't I fight for mine?"

"Because you sold it. It's not for you to have back," Elric barked, his manner no less bitter than before.

"The third man forwards might have a chance. Question is, who's going to be the first and second?" Vintnor displayed the spear and axe theatrically, to prove his point, but far from anyone attempting to seize him, an area around him cleared of people, allowing him a clear path to the marshes.

As Vintnor turned his back upon the villagers, walking away with an air of contempt, Isena quietly hissed at Elric. "There goes our hope, you bloody fool."

Chapter 10

Vintnor had walked from the village as a free man. The tales of his skill with a spear had been repeated and exaggerated to almost supernatural proportions. The fact that the villagers had witnessed Treen fall to his axe, had confirmed his status as a warrior. The idea of pursuing him into the marshes was never considered, yet the notion that they, as a defensive force felt unable to take on one man, highlighted their own frailty.

Vintnor hadn't anywhere specific to go. His home was far from there, its location lost to his mind, amongst the many places Maldred had travelled. As he walked, he tried to picture their faces, first gathered by the hut fire, then his siblings playing in the forest. Their memory brought him joy, more so still, that they were surely safe, due to his actions. He tried to dispel from his mind just how unlikely it was that he would ever see them again.

He'd not walked far, but to navigate in the thick reeds was close to impossible. With the sun all but lost to the clouds and a wall of reeds and occasional silver birch trees, he relied upon keeping a straight path to avoid losing his way entirely, his desired destination simply being dry land.

As he continued, his strategy changed. He found deer tracks. Regularly trodden paths, used by the deer herds to move in comparative safety. These were animals he knew; animals he had studied. He knew those paths would take him efficiently, to better ground. They might even earn him a meal.

His mind continued to drift. He remembered the months he had spent with Maldred and Lind. Though he was every bit a slave, they hadn't been as bad as they could have been; as bad as some of Maldred's customers. He couldn't now think of them, without remembering their savage attack on the boat, and the spear that had taken Lind. It was indeed the work of the spirits; most specifically, fear of the spirits.

His daydream was broken by the sound of movement on the path ahead. He instinctively crouched down, amongst the reeds. Be it a deer or a boar, the idea of hunting again, as a free man, delighted him.

He waiting, controlling his breath, as the splashing amongst the reeds persisted, getting only slowly closer. This was the most natural thing to him. It was nothing to hide for a day, or a moonlit night, in anticipation of just a spear shot at an unsuspecting deer.

When he began to hear words, his mindset changed again. Though the marshes were heavily occupied, he knew there was a chance he may yet need to fight for his freedom.

The first thing that came into sight was an upturned boat, appearing to levitate through the dense reeds. Only as it became perilously close, did he see the body and legs of the two men carrying it. "You've a long way to carry that, before water," he commented, startling the two unarmed fishermen.

"Where, by the spirits, did you come form," the particularly long haired man, at the front complained, as they all but dropped the boat from their shoulders.

"Passing through," Vintnor replied. "From the forests of the middle lands," he added, to put any questions from their minds, before they were asked.

Vintnor had no understanding of just how much he stood out, in a land dominated by farmers and fishermen. To be carrying a spear, would make him a hunter. To be carrying an axe; some kind of craftsman, but to carry both, that was the rarest of things; a warrior.

"Well, to pass through these lands, our Thane will want to meet you, you having travelled so far and all. Just a matter of politeness." They spoke only after sharing a series of concerned whispers. "It won't take long, and our lord will surely feed you before you carry on your way."

As he was led along the short track, back to the village of Hathpit, Vintnor felt his new found freedom ebbing away. Already he was being taken somewhere he didn't want to go, for reasons he neither understood, nor trusted.

Hathpit stood on dryer land, with some worthwhile farmland, but still the presence of boats and fish traps told a story of a close link to the river. The stench of cooking eel, combined with the unique odour of decaying fish, confirmed to his senses that this was still a fishing community, but the boar hanging on a tripod, at the front of one of the roundhouses, and a hurdle pen of sheep, at the back, suggested a more diverse wealth.

"Our lord welcomes you," the man who had done all of the talking said, as he returned from the Thane's roundhouse. "We would ask that you leave your weapons."

Vintnor nodded graciously, but he felt increasingly uncomfortable. He paused before entering the roundhouse, looking around, at the people of the village. They were doing their best to go about their business, but their eyes and their minds were entirely focused upon him.

"Don't mind them," the man assured him. "The last time they saw men of your kind, their village was raided and their food stolen."

"What is my kind?" Vintnor asked, not with anger or offence, but concern.

"You stink of death, worse than a dead hog in the summer sun," the man replied, guiding him into the Thane's house with a gentle push.

Stepping into the Thane's roundhouse felt like stepping into a different dimension. The brightness of the day was instantly lost to a world of shadows, cast by a large fire, and those gathered around it.

Four figures sat around the fire, all facing him, awaiting his presence, as if he were entirely the focus of their meeting. Two of the figures were partially obscured by the shadows, deliberately seated back, away from the fire, as if to highlight their lower standing. Between the two, a rounded face shone, as it reflected the firelight.

It took Vintnor a few seconds for his eyes to adjust. He struggled to make out the difference between the round faced man's body and the massive heap of furs and cloth that he sat on. A slight breeze increased the fire for a few seconds, giving better light, to see the dainty young woman, no older than Andura, perched to his side. She was wearing only the flimsiest of dresses, exposing more flesh than it covered; an ornament, or an item of wealth.

"Well boy, let's be hearing it," the fat man demanded.

Vintnor stood, blank for a few seconds. He was conscious of the fact that two armed men blocked the exit, but he didn't look back, in fear of provoking them. "Passing through, Lord," he eventually replied, unsure of what the Thane wanted to hear.

"A raider then... Break his skull and feed him to the pigs," the considerably obese Thane ordered the men behind him.

"No," Vintnor pleaded. "I've come from Fengate." He turned, holding his hand up to appeal for the extra seconds it would take the Thane to consider his words. The boatman, who had walked him to the village stood, brandishing an axe, ready to strike.

It only took a gentle nod from the Thane to postpone the killing. "You're not of Fengate, else you'd know not to claim to be so, in this house." The Thane looked to him inquiringly, as if expecting something specific. "Who are you, boy?"

Vintnor panicked. There was bad blood with Fengate, that much he could tell, probably enough to get him killed. Alternatively he could be killed as a straggler from Stromgalee's raiding party. "Slave. I'm a slave," he spluttered, realising the truth was the most likely story to keep him alive.

"Let him speak," the Thane instructed his men as he tore a fist full of meat from a roasting pig thigh. "How'd you come to be in a turd sack like Fengate?"

"My master was a trader, Lord. We were there when it was raided."

"That's him, Lord. The True Spear," one of the men beside the Thane said, over obligingly, while the other just nodded in agreement. Vintnor couldn't make out their faces clearly, but he guessed them to be the two men in the boat, at the time he killed Lind.

"I'm just a hunter, Lord," Vintnor insisted, keen to be moving on and concerned for the Thane's interest in him.

"You were a slave, now you say you're a hunter," the Thane said smugly, spluttering through a mouthful of meat. "Which is it, a hunter or a slave?"

"Born a hunter, Lord, made a slave."

"Hmm. A slave is a slave." The Thane held his arms out to the side, to be helped to his feet. The two men to his side, hurried to help. Vintnor watched as they heaved the giant carcass of a man to his unsteady feet. They were nervous; afraid of the Thane, suggesting to Vintnor that he too should be cautious.

Vintnor stepped back and watched as the fat, middle aged man made his way to the door, shaking off his two helpers, before he reached the door, in a vain and unsuccessful attempt to look less feeble.

Though he should have thought many things, including 'how do I get out of this situation?' Vintnor was struck by the quantity of food it took for a man to reach such a vast size. He looked back to the Thane's young wife, tending to the fire. She was shaped like a stick. These weren't wealthy people, or particularly well fed people. As the Thane steadily made his way out, into the open, Vintnor came to the conclusion that he could only be a hated leader.

"Come on then, Slave boy. My people wish to see you... The mighty True Spear!" As he boomed his instruction, the two men from the roundhouse ran behind him with his large pile of furs, like a mobile throne. "I offer you the young man, touched by the Sun God. The True Spear."

The Thane clapped his hands impatiently, looking past the gathered crowd. Two men were wrestling with some sort of beast, in a pit. Vintnor watched, already having guessed that whatever the creature was, he would be expected to kill it, to prove his worth.

Amongst a cloud of mud and dust, a sorry specimen of a man appeared, with ropes pulled tight around his neck. Heavily bearded and covered in filth from head to toe, be looked barely human as he was dragged towards the Thane.

"A Northern Alluni... Curious beasts, aren't they," the Thane said, prodding the wretched man with the point of his sword. As the point of the sword touched the man's ripped tunic, he lunged at the Thane, snapping with his teeth, like an angry dog. "You see, such an animal can't be kept alive. What's worst, it was caught stealing Hathpit crops."

Vintnor looked deep into the Alluni's eyes. He was angry, and he stank of his own excrement, but he wasn't mad. There was something pitiful about him, like a boar, hunted to the point that it refused to run any further.

Though he already knew what was expected of him, his spear being placed into the palm of hand, whilst the tip of another was held to the back of his neck, confirmed the choice he must make.

"These people wish to follow the True Spear into battle. They would reap the rewards the great Sun God has bestowed upon us, but first they must see what you are able to do." The Thane sent one of the men from the river out, along the long open section of ground beside the roundhouses, with a marker stick, to estimate the distance in which he had seen Vintnor kill Lind.

The distance was considerably further; an exaggeration, inflated yet more for the number of times the story had been retold.

"The river's not even that wide," Vintnor complained. "And I hunt animals, not people."

"Yet you have made light work of two warriors since you came up river... With the help of the Sun God, you'll knock him down at the post."

Vintnor solemnly nodded, accepting the only action that would see him alive at the end of it. Two more men, armed with spears stepped forwards, primarily to ensure that the Alluni did indeed run, and also to protect the Thane.

"This is not the will of any god or spirit. This is a man at play," Vintnor suddenly argued, struck by just how different this killing would be.

"This contest is the will of Thane Colos. Which one of you lives and which one dies is in your hands, and the hands of the Sun God, who guides your hand."

Vintnor looked to the earth between his feet. He had heard Maldred talk of Colos the Three, so called because he was as wide as three men. Maldred had also spoken of the cruelty of the man and his greed, only curbed by his own laziness.

The earth by Vintnor's feet was damp and dirty. Pig dung, sticks and even fish scales carpeted the ground around the village. It was as if Thane Colos' laziness had infected his people. Vintnor placed a short log of wood by his feet and knelt on it with one knee. "I need space for this," he demanded of the man holding a spear to his neck.

Colos nodded smugly, for the man to take a single pace back. He struggled to contain his joy, that Vintnor had given in, to such an extent that he looked back to his people expectantly, for the praise and gratitude they were obliged to give.

Vintnor's focus was entirely on the open ground ahead. This was to be the most difficult shot of his life. If it had been a deer, in the wood, he wouldn't have attempted it, but this was his shot at life; maybe even a free life.

"Set him free," Vintnor called, his vision entirely fixed on the marker post. He shut out entirely, the cheers of the gathered crowd behind him. As the Alluni approached the marker post, he focused his mind and eye, first on the centre of his back, then specifically on the back of his head.

The Alluni was still more than ten feet from the marker post, when Vintnor made his move. He dropped the spear and gripped the log beneath his knee, raising to his feet as he did so. Now his mind and eye were as one. He threw the log, with considerable spin, his vision entirely fixed on the back of the Alluni's head, as if he were trying to think the log to its target.

The crowd behind him gasped and muttered, as the Alluni tumbled to the ground, only a foot beyond the marker post. They had witnessed the impossible, but they dare not cheer. They felt the spirits were amongst them, or the Sun God even. They were afraid, now more than ever. They feared a power greater than Thane Colos, and they feared where this new power would take them.

"Well, my people, it turns out the True Spear should be known as the True Log," Colos boomed, playing for his crowd. "Led by the True Spear, we will overcome all our enemies. We will be great."

Vintnor watched the gathered people. They were certainly more warrior like than those of Norsea and Fengate, but their fear was there to see. It was what made them who they were, a life lived in the considerable shadow of one man. A tyrant.

Colos uttered to the man who had been holding the spear to Vintnor's neck. Vintnor didn't hear the words, but the man's actions told him enough. He immediately made his way towards the Alluni, still armed with the spear. Vintnor ignored the words that Colos was spouting to his people. He simply wasn't interested. Instead he followed the spear man as he approached the Alluni. The man's purpose was clear; he had been ordered to dispatch the immobilised Alluni.

The man was Colos' personal guard, a man used to doing the oppressive Thane's dirty work. He quite casually approached the Alluni, raising his spear to kill, without a second thought. He was of a hefty build, and well muscled, but as Vintnor twisted his spear around in a half circle, forcing the handle into the back of his leg, he lost all balance. It was the second shock for the people of Hathpit, in as many minutes, to see the Thane's henchman so belittled.

"You all have the fight of your lives ahead. Do you really want to be killing able bodied men?" Vintnor boomed as he pressed the tip of the henchman's spear hard to his throat.

"That man is an Alluni. A thief, caught stealing our crops... His place is to die, lest we'll have his whole tribe thieving from us," Colos shouted back, his voice quaking with anger.

Vintnor pushed the henchman entirely to the ground and grabbed the Alluni brutally, by the arm. He pointed out three lines burnt into his arm. "He's not an Alluni. He's not anything." Vintnor threw down the spear and pulled up the sleeve of his tunic to expose almost the same mark. "It's the mark of a slave. A slave isn't of a tribe, only property of one!"

Colos scowled for a moment. He could, for the first time, see the dangers of the game he was playing. By hailing Vintnor as a tool of the Sun God, he made him powerful. This was a power he needed to keep control of, if his ambitions were to be realised. He shuffled forwards. His ability to walk was limited by his immensely over loaded frame. He waved his hand for another of his servants to follow him.

The Alluni struggled to his knees, daring to look Colos in the eyes. He continued to stare, not blinking, even as Colos took a sword from the belt of his servant. It was only then that Vintnor realised the situation he had put Colos in. His rule had been undermined. He had been humiliated in front of his people, Vintnor's power appearing greater than his own.

With as much thrust as he could muster, the Colos forced the tip of his sword into the belly of his henchman, slowly pressing it deeper, using his great weight. "With the time you have left, think on the way you failed your Thane... Only the crows have a use for your like." He drew his sword back, deliberately not completing the kill. "You're my property now, you both are... Curse it, you all are," he yelled angrily, barking at his people like a savage dog.

Vintnor obligingly followed him back to his roundhouse, closely followed by the sword bearer. "So, True Spear, what would you have me do next?" Colos spoke with contempt, still enraged by what he saw as a challenge to his power.

"Such matters aren't for a lowly slave, Lord," Vintnor said, understanding at last, just how dangerous Colos was.

"You'll be leading my warriors. You must have an opinion. You seem to like your opinions!"

"I would send someone to Thane Elric, to combine our strength against Stromgalee... If they raided here at the same time as they raided Fengate and Norsea, they must be more than he knows."

At last Colos smiled. The idea of further harm coming to Fengate filled his heart with joy, such was his loathing for Elric. "Then they would run. We don't want them to run," Colos said smugly. "Do you know what we want them to do?"

"To fight, Lord," Vintnor replied obediently, such was clearly the way of slaves and free men alike, in Hathpit.

"Die, boy. We want them to die, especially the pig, Elric... Let them fight. Let them weaken Stromgalee, and I will have this marsh, and the spirit lake, the river even." Colos looked around the house, his anger looking for a new purpose. "Can a man not have something to sit on," he yelled as his young wife entered the roundhouse.

As Colos' pile of furs was being reinstated by the fire, by his wife and another quite down trodden and put upon woman, Vintnor allowed his mind to drift back to Fengate. He first pictured Andura in his mind's eye, as she was when he first met her, driven only by kindness, rather than jealousy and aggression, as he'd seen from her later. He then thought of the wider village. They were what he desired to be most in life; truly free. From that his mind went back further, to his own home village and his childhood; again free people, until the hunger came.

"Well, True Spear, do you see what I see?" Colos exclaimed, breaking Vintnor's daydream.

"I'm sorry, Lord, what is that?" he replied, appearing startled that he was even still in the room.

Colos huffed, but he seemed more relaxed by Vintnor's more vague attitude; less threatened by it. "Do you think it is just chance that the raider shit has been attacking the villages along our river?" he asked, before continuing without allowing Vintnor to answer. "No. We have long been detached from any tribe. No chief to protect us, or to tax us. The Alluni to the North won't venture into the marshes, and the same with the Graftans, to the South, our land acts as an untouchable barrier, which keeps them from fighting. Now the shit, Stromgalee raids to weaken us, to take this land for himself. Either we defend it under a chief or we suffer him as our Chief."

"And you plan to be that chief!" Vintnor added.

"Why in the name of all the spirits not? Elric, the pig, has blocked our direct route to the river for years. We can't allow it to be him, and Consada hasn't got the head for it, I hear," he laughed, tearing into another fist full of meat.

"It can only be you, Lord," Vintnor agreed, patronising the Thane's inflated ego.

Vintnor bowed and began to withdraw from the roundhouse, prompted by the uncomfortable sight of Colos' bloated hand, disappearing beneath his young wife's dress.

"Know this, True Spear. If you deliver me this land, you will have your freedom, and more, so much more, but Elric the pig, needs to be dead before any of that can happen."

"Yes, Lord," Vintnor replied, as he hurried from the house, just as the dainty young woman's dress was being dragged over her head, exposing every inch of what should have been private flesh.

"Tool of the Sun God, is it?" the long haired boatman, who had first brought him in asked facetiously.

"Vintnor will do fine," he replied as the two mutually gripped wrists to confirm both a potential friendship, and more importantly to Vintnor, that one was not more superior than the other.

"Alhart!" the boatman said proudly and boldly. "Not wanting to speak out of turn to the mighty True Spear, but do you plan to let that continue?" Alhart pointed to a peat cutting, on the edge of the village. The Alluni was being wrestled in the water by two men, while a third prodded him with a rough cut spear, every time he attempted to fight back.

"Shall we test our Alluni friend's metal?" Vintnor said with a wry grin.

"A day of entertainment," Alhart replied with glee.

One of the men was attempting to forcibly shave the Alluni with his knife, while the other tried to restrain him, holding him under intermittently, in an attempt to subdue his manic resistance.

"If the bastard is to live, he needs to smell better," one of the two men in the pit shouted, anticipating Vintnor's disapproval.

Vintnor grinned broadly, but did not speak. Instead he gripped the sharpened spear, held by the third man. Once more he grinned playfully, suggesting a sporting contest. Be it as a matter of respect for the True Spear, as the people of Hathpit had come to know him, or out of interest in the potential entertainment, the third man released his hold on the spear.

Vintnor's eyes met with the Alluni, somehow conveying what was to happen next. The Alluni shook his arm free. With his face half shaved and his blood pumping from rage, he looked more than ever like a savage dog. He reached out, catching the crude wooden tipped spear as Vintnor threw it. In one single motion, he jabbed it into the shoulder of the man with the knife, causing a small injury, but crucially, causing the man to drop the knife. The second man attempted to regain his grip, but as he did so the Alluni first struck his ribs with his elbow, then with the handle of the spear.

With unexpected speed, the Alluni turned the spear, thrusting it to the second man's throat. It was an action that would have undoubtedly killed him, but for Vintnor jumping into the water and seizing the handle of the spear, at the last possible second. "We might need him yet, my friend," Vintnor said, once more fixing eye contact to assure the Alluni of his best intentions.

Slowly, and without so much as a blink of the eye, Vintnor released the spear. The Alluni was still in a rabid state. It was an action that could have so easily gone wrong, but it was an act of trust, which after a few tense seconds, the Alluni accepted, throwing the spear into the water.

Vintnor extended his arm in friendship, whilst entirely ignoring Colos' men. "Vintnor," he exclaimed, as introduction.

The Alluni looked at each of the other three with contempt, before accepting his hand with a firm grip of the wrist. "I am Hob," he replied with a thick, gravelly accent, typical of the more Northern tribes.

"You've used one of those before," Vintnor said joyfully, impressed with his skill with the rough cut spear. "Our friend here plans to feed us. Isn't that right Alhart."

Alhart was a man of close to thirty. A fisherman, a farmer, much the same as rest of the village, but he had a mischief about him. It was a trait Vintnor had seen in men before, as if he was trapped in a world too small for him.

Alhart led them into his roundhouse, on the edge of the village. Corn grew on both sides of the path, and pig root, but they grew wispy and poorly kept. Broken fish traps stood piled, waiting to be fixed, and an old split log-boat lay rotting in the earth.
  Hob cast a wry glance to Vintnor, as if to silently comment on the rough state of the place, to which Vintnor grinned briefly before straightening his face to avoid offending his host.
  A boy of about five suddenly ran from the door, followed by an older girl, chasing him. "Yours?" Vintnor asked.
  "No. My sister and her husband live here, with us. They've got another one somewhere abouts." Alhart beckoned them in enthusiastically. "My mother, Neta," he said, gesturing to an older woman, sitting at the back of the house, scraping a hide clean with a flat stone.
  They nodded politely, to the old woman, who stared for a while, before returning her attention to her work, without speaking.
  "What do you know of bees?" Alhart asked as he excitedly produced an earthen flagon from amongst various pots and plates, inside the doorway. Both Vintnor and Hob looked back blankly, bewildered by his question. "They make honey!" Alhart said with increasing enthusiasm, as he laid out three small bowls.
  "Honey is good, if the little bastards don't sting you for taking it," Hob agreed.
  "Oh, it's not honey," Alhart exclaimed pouring a helping of the liquid into each of the bowls, the bowl nearest himself being the fullest. "Drink."
  Vintnor noticed the old woman was once more staring, with a decided frown this time. He tentatively sipped the sugary liquid, before supping it with greater vigour. "What is it?"
  "It makes a fool of a man, that's what it is," the old woman interrupted.

"A gift from the spirits of the trees," Alhart insisted, to the annoyance of the old woman, who wearily rose to her frail feet and left the house, without another word.

The three continued to talk, and drink, becoming increasingly merry. They spoke of the lives they had led, and of their homes and families. It was a process that propagated trust between them, aided by the effects of the alcohol. Eventually they dare to speak of Colos and his plans to become Chieftain, without fear of betrayal.

"What are our chances of seeing the other side of this," Alhart asked, tentatively changing the subject to his requirements.

"If they have sixty of the men that raided Fengate, we haven't a chance, not unless we join with Fengate and Norsea," Vintnor assured him.

"That will never happen," Alhart said, grinning at the thought of such an impossible alliance.

"If he so hated the Fengate Thane, why hasn't he already attacked?" Hob asked as he tipped the last drops of the mead into his bowl.

"Norsea, and a few other villages. They don't like Elric, but they know what Colos the Three would do with such a strategic village." Alhart wobbled to his feet, blundering, before regaining himself. "I have more," he said, producing another flagon, hidden amongst a pile of furs.

"You are truly a man of greatness," Hob exclaimed, holding his bowl out for more.

"What if we attacked them at the river, before they had their feet on land?" Vintnor said, with a new, more serious tone.

"The Three would never allow that... He'll die a happy man, just knowing Elric went first."

"Elric's people won't touch them. We'll face the lot on our own, and they will kill us, all of us," Vintnor said, clearly and sternly, to get his point across, his mind firmly fixed upon Andura.

There was a brief silence, before Alhart burst into laughter. "Best we get this drained then," he slurred hysterically, as he refilled Vintnor's bowl. "Besides, if we attack them at the river, Fengate will lose the surprise. Stromgalee will be expecting a fight."

Hob paused his drinking. He looked directly forwards for a moment, consumed by his own thoughts. "What if someone else attacked the raiders, at the mouth of the river?"

"you'd fool him twice?" Vintnor said, fascinated by the idea.

"Why not. The village of Estrana, at the mouth of the river. The Alluni claim an alliance with them. Some say control... Your raider must surely be expecting to tangle with Alluni, if he raids that piece of river."

"Sod that," Alhart exclaimed. "The Alluni fight naked. I don't fancy leaving my spare limb on the battlefield."

"A bit of paint. Shout the right shit. I'll make Alluni of the lot of you," Hob said cheerfully.

"And I can wear my tunic?" Alhart asked, engulfed by genuine worry, clutching his groin at the thought of the likely injuries.

"Of course. Only a few of them fight bare anyway, to show contempt for their enemies."

"The Three will never agree, anyway. He has his mind made as to how this is going to go," Alhart argued dismissively.

Vintnor purposefully placed his bowl by the fire to indicate he was drinking no more. "I think you are both right... I also think our great leader would allow us to take his warriors for practice and exercise. Scatter Fengate's sheep, while they're distracted. That should convince him."

"You know he'll do us in, win or lose, if we try to fool him," Alhart said, with concern, but also with a tone of rebellion.

"He's got to catch us first. He doesn't look so fast to me," Vintnor joked as he stood up, struggling to maintain full control of his legs. "Might give it a little while before I talk to him, though!"

Chapter 11

The idea of a bodiless burial was to Idenica, too demeaning to consider, for Consada. As such a hastily prepared funeral pyre was arranged, much of the wood being taken from the partially burnt roundhouses of Norsea.

With the constant threat of attack, attending the funeral on Norsea soil was uncomfortable for Elric. The alliance between Fengate and Norsea was however, so important that avoiding the event was never considered.

"Did they really need that much wood for one wooden head?" Elric whispered to Isena, who in turn scraped her foot brutally down his ankle, causing him to call out in pain.

The Seer glared at him for the interruption as he began the ceremony. He chanted praise to the spirits, whilst brandishing a bears skull, seeped in blood. For the seer to conduct the funeral rights was a great honour, usually not permitted outside Fengate. It was part of Elric's attempt to charm Idenica; a ploy undermined by his inability to contain his joy, as the flames began to lap Consada's head, making it glow against the night sky, before entirely engulfing it.

Andura stood one pace back from her parents, as a matter of routine protocol. She had barely spoken to them since Vintnor left Fengate. It wasn't that she was to be offered as gratitude to the spirits. She knew, as her mother did, that Elric would find a way around that. What reviled her was the fact that her planned wedding to Dalric had been moved forwards, again as appeasement to Idenica, and to secure Elric's status as Thane of the combined villages.

Even at his own father's funeral, Dalric found the need to leer at Andura across the flames and smoke of the pyre. She made eye contact with him briefly, before looking away sharply, sickened by the knowledge that he was to be her husband.

Only Idenica remained at the pyre, after the ceremony, watching as flames degraded to smoke and ash, representing the end of all that was familiar to her. The rest of the Norsean people quietly withdrew, but they surely felt a similar sense of uncertainty.

Elric and Isena returned promptly to their log-boat, where Andura was already waiting, slumped down in the shadows of the reeds, to avoid the attentions of Dalric. "Could you not be nicer, my dear? Yound Dalric has just lost his father," Isena said in an unusually sugary tone.

Andura wasn't of a mind to talk. She continued to sit, slumped in the bottom of the boat, considering the days that were to come, and how hopeless every possible outcome was to her.

On the Fengate shore, much was being prepared. Those with fighting skills were teaching their wives and older children the basics of combat; sometimes with proper weapons, but more often with sharpened antlers and clubs.

"Vintnor was right. You should have sold me to Stromgalee," Andura blurted, as they reached the Fengate mooring. "Now you're going to get these people killed to defend me, only to whore me to Dalric of shit festering Norsea."

"Andura. You know it isn't as simple as that," Isena, whispered, trying to prompt her to keep her voice down.

"No, you've both got a sniff of power," Andura deliberately yelled. "But I doubt anyone else will smell it over the stench of fish guts on your hands, you stupid old fools." She ran from the boat, never once looking back.

She had no destination in mind. Her priority was to avoid her parents and their plans for her dutiful future. As she headed away from the Thane's roundhouse, she was struck by the activity; humbled by it, even. As well as the truly hopeless weapons practice, personal possessions and valuables were being moved. Eldwan and his wife lugging an old fur, in which his tools were wrapped. She stopped to watch as they cast them amongst the reeds, before covering them in clods of earth and branches.

The idea of the carpenter, upon whom much of the village's trade had long depended, casting his tools away, intensified her sense of hopelessness. She looked around her, to the people, the village, every boat and pig shed, which made the village what it had always been. She knew then, whatever the result of Stromgalee's attack, it would never be the same.

She took a corn flagon from an old lady, who was attempting to carry two. "Wouldn't want you dropping it," she said kindly, to which the old lady bowed slightly, before carrying on. "Did my father do right?" She asked as the old woman carried on ahead. "Not letting the raider take me... Should he have let me go?"

The old woman stopped and looked at her thoughtfully. "Certainly he did right, else I'd have had to carry these bloody jars on my own," she said, before carrying on her way.

Andura smiled, confused by the old woman's simplified take on the situation, and delighted by the fact that she at least didn't blame her for the situation. Andura looked on as the old woman scraped a hole in the driest piece of earth that she could find, to bury the grain. Quietly, without saying another word, she placed the jar beside the old woman and turned, back to the Thane's house.

It was a tradition that spanned back generations, to gather the precious goods of a village in times of attack and defend them at the Thane's roundhouse. The fact that they planned to fight in the marshes, changed little as it was still the one house that wouldn't be burnt.

Elric looked on as furs and jars were disorderly crammed into his home, by a procession of people. "Can you stack those?" he asked with dismay as pots and leather bags were randomly strewn across the floor.

"Father," Andura said sheepishly. "I don't like the idea, but I will marry him."

Elric smiled softly, cheered by the notion that just one of his problems was a little less. "He won't be so bad. You see. Maybe he just needs a good woman, to make him less of a turd."

She nodded politely, to please Elric, but she knew Dalric represented misery to anyone he called wife. Andura could at last see the pressure Elric was under, and more than that she felt responsible. "I'm going to help people with their things," she announced, to excuse her leaving again so quickly. The truth was that she just didn't know what to say, or who to say it to.

She stood in open ground at the front of the house, looking around for a purpose. Everyone seemed to be busy, either with weapons practice or hiding property. She looked further, beyond the fish traps, where a fire was burning fiercely. The silhouette it highlighted was a familiar one. As she approached, the stench of cooking swine flooded her senses, but it wasn't being cooked in the usual manner, gently in the flames. It was hung over a pot, allowing the fat to drip from its carcass.

Andura watched from a distance, taking in what she took to be another ritual. Eleena ripped strips of cloth as she watched the flames devour the pig. She stood upright and elegant in a long ceremonial gown, her head bowed as her mind travelled to unimaginable places.

"Join me," she said suddenly, without looking around.

Andura stepped forwards cautiously. Eleena had been her friend from her earliest days, but to interrupt a ritual was considered dangerous.

"I didn't mean to," she began, before being halted by Eleena raising an arm, though still not turning back from the flames.

"You disturb nothing," Eleena said vaguely, seemingly mesmerised by the flames. "The company would be good," she at last added as she looked back to her briefly, before returning her gaze to the fire. "I see bits, just shadows, suggestions of what might be," she explained as she once more stared deeply into the flames. "When my grandfather joins the spirits, I will see what he sees. I will see the misery approaching."

"Can you see my... what I mean is, do you see?.." Andura stuttered from the fear of knowing her own future.

"Only suggestions and shadows," Eleena said solemnly. "But you don't need to be a seer to see that."

"Do I have choices? Can you see that?"

"There are many paths... The question my grandfather would ask is, do they all lead to the same place?" Eleena smiled as she spoke, to make light of her words, and more than that, to suggest that she knew something more. Eleena dipped the lengths of cloth into the jar of liquid pig fat, dipping them down, deep into the sticky goo. "The path you might want to take right now would be to the oaks. That is unless you would prefer the shitty path." As she spoke, she pointed out Dalric, who seemed to be discretely searching the village for her. "You'd better go, before he sees you."

Eleena walked away to meet Dalric, before Andura could ask any more. She stepped seductively with the fire behind her, appearing as if she had stepped straight from the flames. "I seek the Thane's daughter, Priestess... I'm told she would be with you."

Eleena stood square on, every aspect of her body language indicating that he was not to pass. "She is not here," she said defiantly.

"A man should be comforted by his future wife on the night of his father's funeral. That's only right." As he spoke, Dalric looked Eleena up and down, without any degree of discretion. Her dress reached almost to the floor, but exposed much of the inside of one leg, something Dalric struggled to see beyond.

He stepped forwards slowly, lowering his hand to her knee, whilst staring her in the eyes, half expecting her to cry out. She continued to stand firm, her eyes glowing with the reflection of firelight. He smiled slightly as he began to move his hand upwards, higher up her inside leg. "Comfort indeed," he uttered as he began to push the last inches of material away to reach his desired target.

"Touch it and I'll see your fingers wither and drop off," she hissed, whilst still staring him in the eyes.

"Your grandfather won't live forever, witch," he snarled, pulling his hand away as if it were burnt, before hurrying back, towards the Thane's house. "Remember, witch," he shouted, clutching his groin as if to make a threat.

Andura made her way to the oaks, considering what she would say to Vintnor, her heart heavy with regret for the bitterness of their last meeting.

The moonlight was shining enough light to guide her way to the oaks, but once she reached them, the vast trees cast the darkest of shadows. She stood, as if entirely blind, allowing her ears to do the seeing. In the distance, the sounds of the village were still clear, and beyond that, wild geese flying by moonlight, but close to her, there was only silence. She felt the discomfort of being watched and the frustration of the unknown. "Who's there?" she demanded, stepping back into the moonlight and the comfort it offered.

The breaking of a branch and the gentle sloshing of feet in water confirmed to her that there was more than one. "Who's there?" she called, more desperately this time.

"Now I see why we're here," came a poorly controlled whisper from the reeds. Swiftly responded to by Hob, clubbing Alhart around the head with reed root, and in doing so, giving up their position.

"Don't mind them. They are going to do very much better when we meet Stromgalee, Aren't you!" Vintnor stressed as he stepped into the moonlight, embarrassed by his inept men.

"We will move like the spirits," Alhart slurred, clearly the worse for the mead, once more.

Andura beamed with delight. "I thought you'd gone. You should have gone, for the things I said, if not my father." She reached out, daring to grip his hand, with both of hers.

"Your father is scared, with good reason... You must take a message to him. Tell him to be sure to meet them in the marshes. We hope to weaken them before they get to you." Vintnor stopped, but it was clear he hadn't finished talking. He looked back to Hob as Colos' men began to emerge from cover.

"What else?" she asked, sensing there was more to tell.

"They raided Hathpit the same night as Fengate and Norsea... Twenty men stayed there the whole night."

"So there's twenty more of them than we knew?" she demanded, immediately realising the significance of what he was saying.

"And we have these men, and more to make that right," Vintnor insisted, proudly presenting the men and women under his command.

"please tell me these men aren't from Hathpit," she said, her voice filled with far greater concern than she had for the knowing of Stromgalee's extra men.

"Unless you all fight together, Stromgalee will rule this land," Vintnor argued.

"Colos the Three would see us all dead," she said desperately.

"We, would see us all live, girl. What our Thane wishes is for another day," Alhart interrupted, speaking as softly and kindly as he could, to assure her of his good intentions.

She looked around, at the thirteen men and three women that surrounded her. They looked to her with expectation, not as an enemy, as she had always been led to believe was the attitude of the people of Hathpit. "These are truly strange and dangerous times," she said uncomfortably, accepting Alhart's words with caution.

"Just make sure he meets them in the marsh. Anything else and Stromgalee will rule us all." Vintnor clutched her hand as he spoke, pulling her closer.

"That would impress your people, wouldn't it!" she said playfully, putting her hand over his mouth as he attempted to kiss her. "Bring me good news and I'll thank you properly," she said, seductively brushing the back of his hand against her groin, just for a second, enough to suggest a promise.

"And she says Colos is dangerous," Alhart muttered, loudly enough to be heard by all present.

"If Elric meets them in the marshes, we will join him there. Meet them in the village and we will see they all have a decent burial," Vintnor stressed, concerned that Elric might still attempt to fight in the traditional manner. His voice was serious, but faltering, his being so taken aback by her suggestion.

"My father won't trust you if he knows Colos is involved."

"He hasn't got to trust us, just to fight with us, not against us."

Andura looked to the people surrounding her. They looked much the same as the people of Fengate or Norsea; people more accustomed to farming and fishing, than fighting. It gave her a sense of confidence, in people she had been raised to never trust. "I'll do my best," she uttered, releasing her grip on his hand. "Now you must go, before you're seen."

Chapter 12

It had been a race of sorts, to reach the mouth of the river, before Stromgalee returned. The situation was complicated by the need to be undiscovered by the people of Estrana, something they would only be able to achieve for a short time.

Their need to avoid the Estranians, and potentially the entire Alluni tribe, led them to a narrow strip of mud and reeds, which was so regularly cut off from land that it was seldom visited.

With the rising sun, so the activity on the river mouth began, forcing them to skulk deeply amongst the reeds, surprise being their most vital weapon.

Hob thrived on a sense of self importance, applying complex symbols and patterns to every inch of exposed flesh, on each of the warriors in turn. As he painted the green dye, he taught them Alluni war chants and even suggested battle tactics, most in keeping with the Alluni.

One woman and one man had agreed to fight naked, a final detail which would surely confirm their identity to Stromgalee, as Alluni. "By the spirits, time we've done, they'll be fighting the Alluni, and leaving us poor bastards alone," Hob declared, delighted by his handy work.

"Only if our raider friend comes by, before we're found," Alhart complained. "Then every bastard will want us dead."

Alhart had been uncharacteristically quiet since their meeting will Andura. Though he had shown the courage to follow Vintnor's deception, he feared Colos, and with family in Hathpit, he felt vulnerable. "Do you really plan to leave that girl and her people to be slaughtered by Stromgalee?"

"That's Colos' instruction. Would you have me betray him?" Vintnor replied, fixed on Alhart's every word and gesture, to gauge his true opinion on the matter.

"That's what I thought." Alhart spoke with surprising disappointment, despite the obvious peril disobeying Colos would bring. "I thought you might be tempted to claim your reward?"

"No. Hathpit has a good number of fine women, and they're all a lot less likely to get me killed... We'll let them blunt their spears on Elric's bones, before we join in, just as Colos ordered."

"You'll go far," Alhart said dryly, before moving away from Vintnor, as a matter of principle.

Hob watched them both, and smirked slightly at their exchange. "Who's to say where the spirits will take us," he said cheerfully, as he continued to paint the warriors.

"One Thane is as good as another," the woman wrapped only in a single large cloth said, with little sympathy for either Colos or Elric. "They all get fat from the sweat and blood of the fools that follow them."

"Elric's not fat. He's as skinny as a weasel," Vintnor joked. "And he stinks of fish guts."

As the day went on, boatmen passed close by, on the river, and foragers came even closer, from the land. There was little doubt that their presence was known. The only question was, how long would it take Estrana to react to the intrusion?

There was little to do but wait. Apart from Hob's paintwork, the only task that did occupy them was the sharpening of bundles of straight hazel wands, which they had cut as they passed through Norsean land. They were far from perfect spears, but, thrown well, they were capable of sustaining a worthy injury.

By late afternoon the number of people in the area began to become a concern. It was as if word was out and those of a mind to, had come along to see.

"Are they going to attack," the woman in the cloth asked, clutching a strangely shaped axe, which looked incapable of killing anything.

"If our friend here is any good with his paintwork, they'll think we're alluni, and leave us alone," Alhart replied as they skulked down flat to the ground, while a log boat passed close to the reed-bed, its occupants showing an unnatural interest in their particular part of the reeds.

"Sooner or later they will come," Hob assured them, his gaze fixed on the boatmen as they headed to open water. With nothing to say or do, and movement even restricted, each of the sixteen watched, transfixed by the actions of the two boatmen as they passed so close by. It was as if they were providing some basic form of entertainment.

As the two boatmen rowed on, to open water, they continued to draw the eye. Their attention was now entirely distracted from the reeds. They were staring out towards the setting sun, as if admiring it, or even honouring it in some way.

"There. Look. Boats," Evali, the woman in the cloth called, pointing beyond the two boatmen. She spoke with excitement, throwing off the cloth to expose her naked, but entirely painted body.

"I see five," a man called from the far side of the group, his voice contrasting to Evali's, quaking with fear of what was to come.

"And another two, beyond that," Alhart announced. "That's seven. That's the bloody lot of them."

"Everyone down. In the water if you have to. We need to hit the last of them, else we'll be fighting the lot," Vintnor instructed, lowering himself almost flat on his belly, as an example to be followed.

The tide was coming in fast, forcing water up the tidal river, and in doing so, propelling Stromgalee's boats. Vintnor knew this was an opportunity, if they could just get the lead boats past and out of range, before they were discovered.

"Would anyone like to tell me what we do if them two give us up," Alhart asked, gesturing towards the boatmen.

"We die horribly!" Hob replied cheerfully, as he followed Vintnor's lead and flattened himself to the damp moss and reed dominated ground.

There was a healthy breeze, blowing in from the sea, and Stromgalee had made every effort to capitalise upon it. He had considered passing Estrana at speed, to be the safest course of action. As such, each of the seven boats were in full sail, and approaching fast.

"I throw the first spear," Vintnor exclaimed, laying down his bronze tipped spear and replacing it with one of the rough cut hazel shafts. "We take the last two," he added, in a quieter voice, as the two boats at the rear became more obviously separated from the others.

"What about them. Do we even know who's side they're on?" the same worried voice asked, who had voiced concerns earlier.

Vintnor looked back, to see a group of eight men, each armed, at very least for hunting. "Ours of course. We're Alluni!" He smiled and signalled for the man to lower himself further amongst the reeds.

The four archers amongst them, each prepared their arrows, selecting their finest for that first, most accurate shot; the best chance of making an early kill. Amongst these was Alhart. He carried the finest, most perfectly fashioned bow, shining, either from use or loving care. "May the spirits guide my arrows," he uttered as the first of the seven boats drifted in fast, still in full sail.

"The mead might," Hob whispered, suspecting he was still the worse for its effects.

As each boat passed, they could see and hear the laughing and goading of the men on board. A fight was underway on the third boat, distracting the rest of the men, even on the other boats. A barbarous voice boomed inaudible words as the boat appeared close to capsizing. It was the voice Vintnor knew to be Stromgalee.

The distraction was the stroke of luck Vintnor's risky plan needed to get the first five boats passed, without detection. The sight of Estranians, watching from the dry ground, offered further distraction; a sight that baffled Stromgalee, but not enough to raise the alarm.

As the last two boats came into sight, the sixteen drew a collective deep breath, waiting for Vintnor to pick his mark. He studied the first, and nearest of the two boats for an easy target. He knew the importance of the first kill, enough to lay down his rough spear and replace it with his bronze tipped fighting spear. A man was reaching up to fold the sail, presenting an unmissable target. This was to be his mark.

He put from his mind the place he was in, the people around him, and any danger he might face. Instead he pictured in his mind a fine stag, drinking from the stream, in the forest lands. His mind and eye were as one as the spear left his hand. He continued to watch the spear as it reached its target, striking the man in the centre of the back, immediately dropping him dead amongst his comrades, in the bottom of the boat.

It took a second for the other men in the two boats to realise they were under attack, and another second for them to do anything about it, by which time they were amongst a hail of rough spears, arrows, and even sharp rocks. Three men blundered into the water; whether injured or just misplaced from panic, was impossible to tell. Axes and spears were launched back, but with the men throwing them, cowering from the onslaught, they were poorly aimed.

Amongst their war chants, the call, "Alluni," from Stromgalee's boat, at the front, confirmed to them that the plan had worked and they believed they were being attacked by Alluni.

Arrows began to cut through the reeds, fired with accuracy, from the five leading boats. Vintnor looked back to see one man laying in the water, and two more with arrows stuck in their flesh.

He hurled another spear, at a single man, still standing on the nearest boat. As his spear struck the man in the thigh, a stricken swimmer caught an arrow, fired by Alhart. "Keep going. Keep the bastards moving," Vintnor yelled at the sight of Stromgalee's five lead boats sailing out of reach.

Alhart fired again, removing another from the second boat, prompting Vintnor to slap him on the shoulder in amazement. "Finish em," he ordered, gesturing towards the single minded, angry men, swimming to the shore, determined to meet them on dry land. "Alhart, can you trim up the second boat, with your bow?"

"Are you planning something stupid," Alhart asked with an air of humour that had been lacking from the man since they left Fengate.

"I want my spear back," he replied, handing his axe to Evali. He began to run through the reeds, parallel to the river. His mind was fixed on the length of rope, trailing behind the empty boat.

"You'll get your stupid self killed," Evali shouted, in an almost obligatory manner, as if offering safety advice, rather than truly caring.

Once level with the boat, Vintnor dived in, without changing speed. He shaped his muscular body as much like an arrow as was possible, demonstrating his experience as not just a swimmer, but a diver.

Darting beneath the water made him a hard target. Alhart's now long arrow shots, increased the difficulty for the three men who remained in the second boat, attempting to fire arrows back.

The gap had widened between the two stricken boats and the five in the lead, Stromgalee being clearly resolved to let them take their chances, for the greater good of the rest of them. Even so, the odd arrow rained down, close to him, from them as well.

It was only as the rope was in his hand that he considered the missing part of his plan; how to actually stop the boat. His weight was certainly not enough, and though the water was not deep, it was deep enough to only allow the tops of his feet to drag on the silty baseless riverbed. The boat seemed to be pulling him under, intermittently depriving him of oxygen, and blunting his senses as it did so.

He cursed his decision to seize the boat as it continued to drag him, relentlessly, towards Stromgalee. From time to time he felt more solid earth beneath his feet, inspiring him to dig his heels in, only to find his leather bound feet dragging through it, as if it were ice on a frozen pond.

Each time he rose to the surface, he would see arrows, fired from the other boats, peppering the water around him, only paused by the first meander in the river. With those few seconds, he saw his chance. It was a natural opportunity to drag the boat into the bank. Aided by a fallen willow tree, laying across the water, he lunged himself into its branches, wrapping the rope as he did so.

Once tied, the boat slid into the bank with ease. Its rough plank hull was bristling with the arrows which had been fired at him, enough to make him consider the stupidity of his own actions.

"True fish, is it?" Alhart joked, between gasps for breath. Behind him the others followed. Evali was now wrapped back in her cloth, inspired not by modesty, but the chill of the water. Trailing behind her, were a much diminished band. Two injured men were each being carried by another two. A woman stood, clutching an arrow, which protruded from her arm, dripping blood from its shaft.

Vintnor watched with anticipation as the last two men appeared from the reeds, each dragging by one foot, the man who had shown such concern, since leaving Hathpit.

"Poor bastard knew this was his day," Vintnor said, placing an arrow in his mud caked hand, as an offering. "We leave him here."

"He must return to Hathpit. His spirit must dwell amongst us," the injured woman argued.

"His spirit will have to find its own way back," Vintnor barked, pointing to a group of Estranians, which now numbered close to twenty.

She glared at him, seething, before looking to the others for support. "They would be the orders of Lord Colos," Alhart assured her. "We need to go, now."

"Who's the fastest?" Vintnor asked, looking over the bedraggled band.

Both Hob and Alhart stepped forwards. "Reckon that's both of us," Alhart said dryly, while Hob's attention was almost entirely drawn by the Estranians, who stood, in an ever more warlike manner, at the edge of the reeds.

"Both of you. Take these weapons and give them to Elric. Give them to him as an act of piece from Thane Colos," Vintnor instructed them. As he spoke, Vintnor frantically gathered together the spears and axes, taken from Stromgalee's men.

"The Three will hang your balls out to dry for this," Alhart said, with a smirk. "And ours along with them."

"Run, and don't stop," Vintnor insisted, as some of the Estranians began to disperse, amongst the reeds.

"Still planning to leave that girl to die, are you?" Alhart asked smugly.

"Go," Vintnor boomed back, gripping his spear as he reached up onto tip toes, studied the movements of the Estranians, over the reeds.

"Do we fight them, True Spear?" the woman with the arrow in her arm asked, looking to him for both leadership and hope.

Vintnor continued to look. He couldn't actually see the fighters, who had been sent into the marsh, only the movement of reeds.

They were approaching from all sides. Not many, but enough to make a mess of the battle worn handful of people he had. His mind was working at an accelerated pace, driven by adrenaline.

He considered the woman's words. She knew his name, yet when she felt vulnerable, she chose to call him True Spear. If the tale of Lind's death had travelled to Hathpit, it may well have reached Estrana. "Take the boat," he eventually ordered. "If I don't get back in time, make sure you meet Stromgalee with your feet on land."

As the others began to load their weapons and their injured into the boat, Evali approached Vintnor. "So, when do we join the battle? Do we wait for Elric to be defeated?"

"Stand by the side of Elric. Anything else and Stromgalee will enslave all of the villages." With those words, Vintnor turned and walked away, into the densest of the reeds. "Spirits be with you," he called as he vanished entirely from sight.

Evali returned her attention to the captured boat, ensuring that everything was aboard in the small amount of time they had left, to evade capture. She looked back through the reeds, and then to each man and woman in turn. "Where?" she demanded. "Where's the missing bastard?" she yelled, already knowing the answer to her own question. The missing young man had run back to Colos. Frightened and with loyalties divided, he represented the dilemma of most of them; he was just the one that did it first.

Chapter 13

It was a curious tactic of the Estranians, sending their people into the reeds, in no particular order, but it made the vast reed-bed a dangerous place to be.

To buy the band time, Vintnor did what he did best; he hunted. He moved slowly and silently amongst the reeds, only stopping when he heard movement nearby. He stood perfectly still, poised to strike. The reeds were the perfect hunting ground, with almost no visibility, it delivered Vintnor's first victim straight to the tip of his spear. With a single powerful thrust forwards, he rammed the spearhead deep into the throat of his prey, taking the weight of the body on the shaft of the spear as the man died in silence.

Such a sudden death caused enough splashing in the inch or two of water, beneath their feet, to attract the attention of two more of the Estranian warriors. Still unsure of what they were hearing, they made their way towards the source of the sound, holding their spears ahead of them, from the hip. They called to each other, to avoid losing their way, and in the process, gave their position away to Vintnor.

A Third man Joined them, calling loudly for the location of his comrades, who had met, only yards away from Vintnor. Vintnor dibbled his fingers in the stinking mud, before wiping them down his face, adding camouflage to his quite striking Alluni war paint.

The two warriors both called to the third man, prompting Vintnor to bob down in a deeper patch of water, soaking him from the knees down. The reeds were moving in two locations ahead of him, the movements of water helping to pinpoint their locations. He decided the first man he saw would get the spear. Leaving him with an axe to dispatch the other two.

As he gathered his breath, awaiting a clear shot, he remembered the spear, dropped by the first man. He swore to himself for not picking it up, considering how much easier his task would have been with two spears. He briefly looked back, in the hope of seeing a clear path to the discarded spear, but every reed looked the same and every footprint was lost to the water.

The quite sudden appearance of not one, but two of the men, startled him. His mind began to run at a hurried pace, and his heart pump at such a speed that he could feel the blood forcing its way through his veins.

With his spear drawn back, ready to strike, he betrayed his every instinct. He slowly stood upright, his eyes piercing in their focus. "You don't know it yet, but you're both corpses if I choose to make you so," he declared.

"Who, under the light of the sun, are you?" the bolder of the two asked.

"The True Spear!" Vintnor replied, counting upon the exaggerated stories having reached Estrana.

"Why should we believe that?"

"Which one wants to help me prove it?" he demanded, drawing the spear back to the point of throwing. "Tell your friend to show himself."

"Hosk. You'd better come hear. There's a dead man standing in front of us," the bold man said, defiantly.

As he spoke, the third man ran from the reeds, roaring like a savage beast, with his spear poised to strike. Vintnor bobbed down and forced his spear upwards, under his ribs. As he did so he twisted the body around to provide himself with a shield against the other two. The couple of seconds it took for the body to hit the waterlogged ground, caused enough hesitation for Vintnor to vanish from sight, amongst the shroud of reeds.

"Perhaps not such a scary name after all," he uttered to himself as he paused to gain some sense of direction. Now only armed with an axe, he considered his best way forwards, or indeed back.

He slowed his breathing, even clearing unnecessary thoughts from his mind. He took in every sound which might give a clue as to the route back to the river. He was too far to hear the water, but as the fuzz cleared from his mind, every sound came into focus. The gentle breeze, blowing in the willow leaves, producing a unique rustle, the sound of teal on the estuary, even the distant mooing of a cow, gave away the direction of dry land.

There was a good chance of running, if he ran then, but what good would it do? That was the question that bothered him. Even his skill with the spear would do little good against the might of Stromgalee's raiders. For that reason he stood, waiting.

The two men were now staying close together, perhaps wondering if his claim to being the True Spear had some foundation. Vintnor was still largely seeing with his ears, pinpointing their location from the sounds of their feet in the water.

He wasn't going to be caught the same way again. He knew they were about to come into view, and planned to gain the advantage. He pictured in his head, a deer, walking beneath a tree, back in the forest lands of his birth. It helped him to contain his fear as he propelled himself with speed, towards the two men, hurling the axe as a clear target came into sight.

As his axe struck the furthest of the two, full in the chest, the bold man threw his spear, but it was a hurried shot, complicated by the reeds and its proximity to its target, allowing Vintnor to twist his body, enough for the weapon to glide past him, with an inch to spare. Vintnor continued his advance, swinging his right arm, as if it were still holding the axe. The blow should have been easy to block, but for the confusion of the situation, which allowed the awkward, but powerful punch to plough into the side of his head. Vintnor followed through with the weight of his body, forcing the man down, into the mud and water.

By now Vintnor had a clear plan in his head, and, as he held the man's face in the mud and water, just to subdue him for the purposes of a calm and reasoned, one sided conversation, he carefully selected his words.

Eventually he pulled the man from the water, allowing him to gasp for air and splutter the mud and water from his mouth. "If your Thane isn't very careful, he's going to miss a great party today," he began, slapping the man's face to see he was fully conscious and understanding. "What you saw on the river was the raider, Stromgalee, going to meet the villages of Hathpit, Fengate and Norsea... Do you know what Stromgalee saw?"

The man looked back at him blankly, enough to inspire another slap to the face. "This! He saw Aluni war paint," Vintnor pushed him back into the mud to fully display the Alluni symbols painted on his arms. "If Stromgalee wins today, there will be a new chiefdom, and he'll be heading for your Alluni arse licking village for revenge."

The man struggled to compose himself, looking back to his dead comrade, with Vintnor's axe protruding from his chest, before cowering lower in the shallow muddy soup. "You see your Thane is going to want to run to the Alluni, who might wander over in a couple of days, after the battle is done, or they might just give up Estrana, in favour of trading with the raider lord. One way or another, you're people are in the shit."

Vintnor stood, offering the man his hand, to help him up. He tentatively took it, looking back again to his dead friend. The man who had previously done all the talking, remained silent. "You might yet be the hero of your village, if you can convince your Thane to join the battle, and see off the raider, before he rules you."

The man nervously nodded. Be it from fear or the cold of the water, his hands were shaking, while he looked up like a chastised dog, through hooded eyes.

"Good man," Vintnor said cheerfully, patting him on the back like a trusted friend. "Now, on your way, before I split you head."

Hob and Alhart had discussed the benefits of returning to Colos, but decided the over sized Thane's brutal, vengeance based approach to justice could go wrong for them, so, with apprehension, they followed Vintnor's instructions.

Despite the urgency of their task, they took a wide ark, around the burnt remains of Norsea, through the all but impassable marshes beyond. They hoped to meet with a less hostile welcome there, with everyone's focus being upon the river, hoping even to meet Andura, rather than armed, scared people, who may not be of a mind to listen.

They crouched amongst the reeds, watching glimpses of the village they could see, considering their best way to present themselves, without getting killed. Their was a gathering at the Thane's house. A circle of people, stood, absorbing the words of a speaker, obscured from view.

"Are the fools going to fight there?" Hob asked as they both tried to make out what was going on.

"Without the sacred fire, a village isn't a village," Alhart argued. "Why would they abandon it on the say so of a man with no village. With no place at all."

"Sounds like you're missing your brew," Hob joked.

"We're in a hornet's nest. That much I know," Alhart said morbidly as he looked for Andura.

As if to confirm his point, two men pounced upon their backs, from the patch of gorse bushes, behind them, forcing their faces into the dirt. "Don't resist. Not unless they look like doing us in," Alhart spluttered as a third man casually walked in front of them.

The third man was Dalric, tasked by Elric, with the demeaning task of guarding the sheep. "Where are the rest of your people? When will they attack?" Dalric demanded, pressing the point of his spear, first on the back of Hob's neck, then Alhart's.

"We're not raiders. We're from Hathpit," Alhart insisted, his voice hurried and interrupted, knowing there was a chance of immediate execution. "We bring weapons, from Colos the Three."

"Do you know what I think... I think Dalric of Norsea single handedly took the first two raiders, while Thane Elric spews his hot air. That's what the people will see." One of the two men, holding them looked up at Dalric in disbelief, while the other man took it as the way of things, pushing Alhart's head forwards for Dalric to impale with his spear.

"They'll be here soon," Alhart blurted as Dalric drew his spear back for a swift kill. "You'd be the man that ignored our warning, and our help... That's what they'll see." He gritted his teeth and closed his eyes tightly, still expecting death to come.

"You have a wise head," Dalric said smugly, after several seconds of torment, Allowing Alhart to anticipate his demise. "Maybe it's not ready for spiking just yet!"

It was with an air of triumph that Dalric and his two companions, marched them into Fengate. It was just the effect Dalric had planned, marking him as Thane material, in the eyes of the combined people. "I offer you the first two heads of the great battle to come... Spies, lurking, counting our numbers for their master."

The two were now dirty and bruised, having been brutally handled, pushed and dragged into the village. "Lord, they are close," Hob pleaded, as Elric stepped forwards. "We are from Hathpit, Lord."

"Yet you wear Alluni paint," Isena interrupted, before Elric could speak.

"Colos of Hathpit sends you weapons as an act of piece between our two endangered villages," Alhart said, looking frantically back to Dalric for the weapons.

"The weapons we captured from you," Dalric said proudly and with the arrogance that made him so widely loathed.

"You lie," Elric snapped at Alhart, enraged by the suggestion that Colos would ever, under any circumstances make peace with him. Elric's anger reflected a deep and long standing conflict between the two Thane's, and it brought out an unfamiliar, vicious side to the man.

Before he could react any further to Alhart's words, Andura stepped forwards, whispering in his ear. Whatever she said seemed to quell his temper instantly, his face reverting back to the more approachable Thane, whom his people had not so much respect, but love for.

"Tell me again," he said, before casting an accusing stare upon Dalric. "The truth this time, or you're eel bait."

"The weapons were a gift, Lord. From Vintnor, the True Spear. He aims to be here for the battle." Alhart shook off Dalric's grip, from his shoulder and took a purposeful step forwards. "We took one of the raiders boats as they joined the river, Lord. That's where the weapons were taken."

"And the paint was to put the blame upon the Alluni!" Elric added with amusement. "How many of you are there?"

"We were separated, Lord. Us and ten perhaps, if they don't go back to Hathpit."

"And what does the sack of shit say on the matter?" Elric asked, his tone changing automatically to emphasise his hatred of Colos.

Alhart paused to consider his reply. "He plans to wait until you are defeated, then, when the raider is at his weakest, he plans to attack."

Elric huffed, acknowledging the problem Colos' plan posed. "And you two men. Will you fight with us, even if it is against your own people."

"You have my allegiance, Lord," Hob announced, standing upright in defiance of Dalric and his two bodyguards.

Elric looked to Alhart, imposing the question upon him once again, without speaking a word.

"I have a family, Lord... I pledge you my last drop of blood against the raiders, Lord," he stressed, nervously awaiting Elric's judgement upon him. He expected the worst. Anything less than mindless devotion, in Hathpit, would see a man dead.

"That's as much as I would ask of you," Elric said, waving a hand for Dalric and his guards to release them.

"Where is Vintnor," Andura asked, before her father could say any more.

"He stayed back to gain us time, from the Estranians," Hob said bluntly. "He'll spike a couple of them and catch us up. Don't worry about him."

"I assure you I'm not. We just need every man, especially the True Spear," Andura added defensively, in response to Dalric's disapproving scowl.

With the knowledge of Stromgalee's approach, the people began to disperse. They had their prearranged positions, in the marsh. Part of a plan that involved the raiders, behaving in the way predicted; separating their forces to gain position upon the village itself.

The seer stood, dressed in garlands of mistletoe; a symbol of his sacred status, and fair warning of the darkest of curses, should any man dare strike him down. He watched the people as they vanished into the marshes, chanting to the Sun God and the spirits of the water for all the good fortune he could muster.

His chants only stopped when the village was down to a handful of people. "Why two?" he asked Eleena, as she prepared the pots of pig fat and cloth, to hide amongst the stacked hoards of the people's possessions, stored in the Thane's house. "The spirits will see your flame doesn't go out. To leave two only shows them doubt."

Eleena smiled. "You are ever wise, Grandfather," she said, looking to him with a question laying heavy on her mind. "I saw those men in my dreams. I've seen them fight along side us. How is that so?"

"I think you already know, my girl. The spirits know what is to be, and what is to not be. It is their mercy that they don't load it all upon you at once."

She looked at him with a tear in her eye and shook her head. "No Grandfather. Not now. Not ever," she insisted tearfully, reaching out to him, only for him to step back from her embrace, such was his way.

The old man frowned back at her, considering her display of emotion to be an unacceptable sign of weakness from the powerful priestess, she must become.

As she continued into Elric's roundhouse, she pulled back in fear, at the sight of Maldred, lurking in the poor light, like a guard dog, threatening to bite.

The fire was largely obscured by the vast piles of day to day goods and food, which had been stored their, working upon the theory that whatever else the raiders did, they would not burn the Thane's house. Even if they burnt every other item of property in the village, the Thane's house would surely be spared the torch, so as to inflict their curse upon the village.

Eleena searched amongst the goods, looking for a worthy spot to place just one of the pots, as her Grandfather had advised. Eventually she found a place, amongst a pile of wooden tools and two poorly dried furs; items she considered the raiders would not care for.

With a small stick, she took the flame from the fire, to the pot. "Spirits, preserve this village, and its people, should that be your will... if it is not, allow us to join you in the unseen world, to feast the endless feast." As she lit the fat coated cloth, she blew hard, causing just a slight smoulder and a hint of smoke, but nothing any man would notice, amongst the smoky haze of the house fire.

"Come on, my friend," Elric said to Maldred, to the sight of the hopelessly crippled trader dragging himself out into the open, having waited for the bulk of the villagers to leave, rather than be seen in what he considered to be such a diminished state.

"I'm staying," he declared, glaring up defiantly, waiting for anyone to argue.

Elric nodded solemnly, understanding fully Maldred's thinking, but as Eleena left the hut she stopped, observing the sorry wretch. He laid largely flat to the ground, his legs dragging behind him like a snake. He had cut his beard to ensure it didn't drag in the dirt, but his face was still filthy, just from its proximity to the ground. He had a single knife, wedged into his belt, close to the middle of his back. He was a man prepared for a dignified death.

"You were granted the insight of the spirits!" she began, in an uncharacteristically strong voice. "You surely understand that if you try and change that future; the path the spirits have set for you, you risk making it many times worse."

Maldred looked at her with fear; a far greater fear than he'd shown Stromgalee, even as he struck the blow that cost him his mobility. His fear and respect for the spirits exceeded that of most men, and such a grim prediction from someone he considered spiritual, terrified him. "I hope to defend my friend's home," he argued, with every bit of colour vanishing from his grubby face, as he absorbed Eleena's warning.

"We must all accept our fate, once the path is set," she said sternly. "To try to make liars of the spirits, will bring your misery tenfold."

"What misery could be more than this?"

Eleena didn't answer. She considered a debate on the matter beneath her status.

"May the spirits embrace you, and the Sun God light your way," Isena said, before turning away sharply, with a tear in her eye.

"Goodbye, friend," Elric added, as they left for the marshes, leaving Maldred alone, in the abandoned village, awaiting his fate.

Chapter 14

"There's a bloody lot of them," Evali observed as they watched the five remaining boats moor in a natural recess in the river, as it took a sharp meander.

"Less than there were," one of the men said proudly. "When do we have another go at them?"

"When Lord Colos orders it... When the rest of Hathpit attack."

"But what about the True Spear?" the man argued.

"He's not here, is he," she snarled back. "For all we know he's gone on his way and left us to it... Couldn't blame him."

The man skulked back into the reeds, displeased with her response, but also powerless to do any different.

They had left the injured a safe distance from any likely battle, reducing their numbers to only eight. Evali knew, even if they were to attack, with Stromgalee's feet on land, they would be quickly slaughtered, and so, she became determined to await a signal of Hathpit's attack.

The wait continued for so much longer than anyone could have expected. Stromgalee's people were strong; strong enough for the element of surprise to be unimportant to him. He seemed to want their presence to be known as they sharpened weapons. Some even stopped to eat. It was a tactic; to give those that would, time to run.

"Bloody well keep down," Evali hissed at the eldest of their number, as he moved to a better position, to see what was going on. "We'll be eel food if the bastards see you."

"Who put you in charge, anyway?" he complained, grudgingly lowering himself to a safer position.

"Did you want to stand in front of Colos The Three and explain our little wander?" she asked.

The man was sufficiently slow witted that his mind could be seen working, conjuring up memories from the past, when Colos' orders had been disobeyed. "Enjoy it while it lasts," he eventually, grudgingly agreed.

"They're on the move," Evali said, relieved to have distraction from the challenge to her self elected leadership.

An ordered group of the raiders could be seen moving off, into the marsh, quickly disappearing amongst the reeds and sparsely placed silver birch and willow trees. Evali watched them, her mind focused upon their actions, and entirely disconnected from those around her, who were whispering amongst themselves, each with a different idea of what they should be doing.

"What are we supposed to do now," the older man asked with an air of smugness.

"Return to Colos. Fight with our village, as we should have in the first place," another man, who have previously remained silent, said.

Evali held her silence. There were, as Vintnor had predicted, two clear groups. The first group moved off, along the river edge, in a direct and predictable route towards the villages of Norsea and then Fengate. The second group set out in what could be assumed to be a wide arc.

She put her head in her hands, for the first time revealing her sense of hopelessness. "All we can do is return to Colos," the man said again, more insistent this time, encouraged by her display of weakness.

She glared at him, defeated. "We're too few," she admitted.

"We're just the right number," came a voice from the reeds, startling the eight, causing each of them to reach for their weapons.

"I bloody near killed you," the older man complained, having taken a feeble swipe with a reed knife, some three feet short of Vintnor's face.

"You were easier to find than they were. You're lucky the bastards didn't spot you," he said, moving next to Evali.

"Should we send someone to Colos?"

"No, he'll have the villages watched well enough. Besides, we need every one of us, if we're going to steal the boats."

"Steal the boats?" she repeated with surprise.

"Your oversized Thane won't let us attack until Elric is defeated. He never said anything about the boats... in fact we'll make a gift of them to him. Should be enough to get you all out of the shit."

The others agreed enthusiastically, each of them fearing Colos reaction to their unauthorised attack on Stromgalee.

Vintnor and Evali moved ahead slowly, keeping a large, fallen willow tree between them and the guards, left behind to protect the boats. "I make five of them," Vintnor whispered.

"And one on the lead boat is six," Evali added, moving up beside him. She looked back to see that the others were far enough back, to talk privately. "You don't give a shit for Colos, do you?"

"Why would I? First chance I get, I'm out."

"You could have run. What holds you back?"

Vintnor just grinned, and moved ahead, towards the fallen willow.

"You hope to hump the Thane's daughter!" she laughed. "You'll be at the end of a long queue, by the time Stromgalee's men have done."

Vintnor grinned again, but continued to study the position of the guards, at the moored boats. They were little more than a spear's throw away, and distracted by their own banter; jeering and laughing as one of them rubbed a handful of fish guts into the face of another.

"We need to wait until the others are further away, else they'll come back," Evali stressed, knowing how hopelessly they would be trapped.

"Sensible," Vintnor agreed, silently directing two men towards a rotted trunk, to their left, and another two into the reed to the right. Before they could take proper position, he ran forwards, shouting loudly, "ATTACK."

"You shit brained fool," Evali called in frustration and anger, grudgingly following him as he ran in full view. It appeared a hopeless distance, but Vintnor hurled his spear anyway, for once missing his target. "Useless pig's arse," Evali shouted, as the guards scrambled for their weapons.

Two arrows passed close by, but it slowed neither of them. The others were still advancing, but through better cover, and slower, held back by mud and water under foot. The six guards formed an ordered defensive line, close to the boats, presenting swords and spears, while a youngster stood wide, with a bow.

Vintnor hurled his axe, without slowing his pace, hitting a man in the stomach, hard enough to knock him backwards. He immediately retrieved his spear, and threw it, all in one smooth, perfectly executed motion, killing a second man instantly.

The archer retreated to one of the boats, firing arrows at speed, while Vintnor and Evali clashed with the three remaining, Vintnor only armed with his bare hands and his considerable strength.

He gripped the spear, held by one of the raiders, holding it horizontally, so as to hold all three back. One man struck Evali with his fist, dropping her to the ground with ease. The three focused their attention on Vintnor, paying Evali no more heed.

She produced from the folds of her tunic, a short, forked piece of hazel, with a sharpened point, which fitted perfectly in the palm of her hand. She jabbed at the men's lower legs, stabbing into calf muscles, dropping and immobilising two of them. She continued stabbing the men as they fell to the floor, killing them both with terrifying speed and brutal vigour.

Vintnor pushed back the third man, with little effort, raising the spear to a position to strike, but before he could thrust the weapon forwards, his intended victim fell to the floor with an axe blow, struck between the shoulder blades, by one of the other men, as they ran from the reeds.

Vintnor composed himself, Taking in his surroundings as the adrenaline rush of battle subsided. Time seemed to be stationary as he once more surveyed the death that surrounded him. He looked up, to see Stromgalee's archer standing; his bow string drawn back.

To Vintnor's left, one of his own men laid on his back, rolling in agony, with an arrow in his chest. To his right, another stood, useless to the fight, frantically trying to pull an arrow from his shoulder.

Vintnor looked again at the archer, who had paused entirely; like him, considering his options. Though the archer's face was partially obscured by his hand, holding back the bow string, the face was familiar.

"Balmoor?" Vintnor uttered in astonishment. He looked to his right, where one of his own men was in the process of arming a captured bow. Without a second thought, Vintnor grabbed the string. "He's not one of them," he exclaimed, tugging hard at the bow to be sure it wasn't fired. "He's a captive, just like I was."

"Let me explain something, pig shit," Evali snarled, engulfed by anger at what she considered Vintnor's betrayal. "If it fires arrows at you and your people, it's your bloody enemy." She looked him in the eyes and gripped his testicles with enough force to effectively paralyse. "Since we met that cursed girl, you've been thinking with these. Do it again and I'll cut them off," she hissed.

When she eventually released her hold, she looked back to the boy. He had bobbed down in the boat, making himself a difficult target, but still sufficiently visible to watch as he drifted down the river, having released the mooring rope in the confusion.

Evali picked up the nearest spear and hurled it with a blind range, but with neither sufficient accuracy nor range. Vintnor held his hand to her face, in the hope of silencing her, only to have his hand slapped away. "What," she barked.

Vintnor grinned, as he picked his axe from the dirt and put his foot on the throat of the man it had injured. "We've done it. Half of the bastards are coming back." Vintnor began hurriedly gathering captured weapons. "Now we run!"

Chapter 15

Stromgalee approached the village with disregard, rather than caution. He saw the people of Fengate as fishermen and herdsmen, and nothing more. As such, when the word reached him of the attack on the boats, he sent Ruke to their defence, with what had been Treen's men, almost halving his attacking force.

They approached along the same almost impassable route, through the marshes, taken by Alhart and Hob, a short time earlier. It came with its own risks, but Stromgalee was not prepared to be caught on open water again.

"Let's get these sheep humpers dead," Stromgalee bellowed as the first of the Fengate roundhouses came into view. His men cheered with one voice, waving weapons in the air. Their blood thirsty chants bellowing across the marshes, to the terrified ears of those who laid in wait.

With the movement of one hand, Stromgalee called for silence, halting the men on the edge of the village. He watched, scanning the houses and buildings for movement. He briefly looked across the marshes, through the thinning reeds, before refocusing his attention upon Elric's house. "The bastards have run," he boomed. Turning, laughing loudly to his men, encouraging them to do the same. He beckoned one of the two men forwards, who were carrying smouldering torches. "We'll see if there's any left," he jeered, as his men began to rummage amongst the stacks of reeds and fish traps expecting to find at least the odd straggler.

Stromgalee and two of his more disciplined men stood back, three yards from the door of the first house, as the roof began to burn. He drew his sword, not for battle, but for sport; his adrenaline up.

"Lord," one of the men called, for his attention, at the sight of Maldred, crawling out, on the open ground, ahead.

"Looks like they've sent their best man," Stromgalee laughed, prompting his men to jeer and goad. "I don't think you have anything left to trade, old man."

"What are you going to do, bite us?" one of his men shouted as he threw a large stone at Maldred, striking his arm with enough force to bruise, but nothing more.

"We'll see an end to this pit of fish shit, once and for all," Stromgalee boomed, picking a leather bag from the dirt. "And when we've taken their homes and their food, we'll hunt them. We'll tear the hearts from their men. We'll fill their women, and enslave their children." He was working his men up, into a frenzy, quite deliberately, ready to send them off in search of the people of Fengate.

While his men burnt a second house, he walked to the mooring, where he reached down and filled the bag with water. "Not worth a shit," he complained as the bag began to leak.

Maldred dragged himself forwards to meet him, with a light cudgel tied to his wrist, allowing him the use of his hands to drag himself along. "Face me!" Maldred shouted, pushing himself up, onto his knees, wincing with the pain the movement put upon his still quite freshly wounded legs.

"Battle of battles," Stromgalee boomed, throwing the bag of water in his face, which in turn caused Maldred to fall over sideways. "All that crawling about in the dirt. The man needed a wash," Stromgalee laughed, inducing a volley jeering from his men. "Nobody is to harm that man," Stromgalee declared in a sudden, stern tone.

He thrust the bag into the hands of one of his men, ordering him to refill it. He drew his sword and purposefully strode to the Thane's house, his two best and most trusted men, joining him, shoulder to shoulder.

The wind leading the coming storm, suddenly picked up, lifting the cloth curtain of the doorway, as if to invite them in. The man to his left; a superstitious type, looked to Stromgalee, as if to silently comment on the eerie event.

"The spirits are with us, my friend," Stromgalee assured him, slashing the curtain with his sword, fully aware that if it were a trap, they would be hugely vulnerable.

Inside, illuminated by the glow of the fire, they saw piles of fur, pots and bags of food, even nets and clothes, anything the people considered important enough to spare from the flames. He took a few steps back outside. "Our friends have gathered their most precious things for us... The spirits are truly with us," he called joyfully, as he was handed the leaking bag of water. "That's not all we want from them, though. For the taking of the Lord Treen, my brother, and yours, we want their lives."

To the jeering and chanting of his frenzied men, he walked back into the roundhouse and doused the fire, causing a great hiss and a cloud of smoke and steam so great that a plume of it puffed out of the doorway.

"Do we wait for the others," the superstitious man asked, his concerns still plain to see, in his every agitated mannerism.

"To hunt a few fishermen?" Stromgalee asked loudly. "Or do you fear their women?"

The man looked to his gathered comrades, and to the darkest of black thunder clouds, behind them. "I fear humping myself to death," he shouted loudly, in the spirit of the occasion, but his discomfort of the omens that he read into the gathering storm, was clear to see.

With the first claps of thunder, Stromgalee ordered his best men to find the tracks, made by the fleeing villagers. This in itself spread his men out, over a wider area than was comfortable. Every footprint in the mud, and every freshly flattened reed, caused his men to dispersed further.

The reeds brought each man's vision down to only a few feet in front of them. No man could see another. Their senses were muddled by the repeated crashing of the storm, and the disorientation of the loss of direction. The occasional splashes of feet in water, being the only sign that they were not entirely alone.

A sudden exaggerated crash of thunder, accompanied by a tremendous flash, against the blackened sky, signalled to those who held with the spirits that they were indeed disfavoured by the Sun God.

From the reeds, a battle cry seemed to reverberate from all directions. A sudden lashing of rain, shook every reed, and muddled the men's senses further. The attacking force were like ghosts to them, only being seen or heard when they wanted to be, appearing upon each man in twos and threes, screaming a shivering battle cry, with every thrust of their often makeshift weapons.

The reeds formed a cloak of deceit; a shroud behind which combat skills accounted for so much less. Amongst these reeds, Dalric stalked, unusually unaccompanied. He hunted not at the front, or amongst Stromgalee's men, but deeper in the marshes, where the willows and the silver birch broke the monotony of reeds.

It was a sacred place, occupied by the spirits, and so, at such a critical time in the existence of the village, it was also occupied by the Seer.

Dalric crept, like a wolf upon a flock, as he sighted the doubled over old man, chanting to an ancient willow tree, which had stood in defiance of the elements for countless years.

Dalric was no spearsman, but his cowardice tempted him to throw the weapon anyway, in the hope of not having to face the spiritual old man.

He drew back his spear, taking a couple more tentative steps forward. His hand shook, enough for him to lower the spear, and adjust his grip.

"Dalric of Norsea," the old man said, quite suddenly halting his chanting. He slowly turned. In contrast to Dalric, he showed no fear. He seemed at ease, as if he was already in the divine place, amongst the spirits.

Once more Dalric's hand shook, more terrified by the old man than he was of Stromgalee or any one of his men. The old man bent his head up, just to look him in the face. There was no anger there, there wasn't the attitude and aggression that the old man so often displayed for little or no reason, and there was certainly no fear.

"Why do you smile, old man?" Dalric asked, nervously taking a few more steps towards him.

"I saw you coming," he replied. "I've been watching your approach my whole life. You are to me, the gatekeeper to their world." The old man shuffled towards him, lowering his head, just for the comfort of his crippled spine. "Don't you have a question for me, before I go?"

Dalric held his spear defensively, as if he were being threatened by a dozen men. "Will I one day be Thane? Will I be a great leader?" he eventually asked, confused and intimidated by the Seer.

The old man took from his belt a handful of tiny stones. He sprinkled them into the water, which surrounded his feet and studied the splashes and rings each stone made as it dropped. "For what is not free, there is a price," the old man said, gripping the neck of Dalric's spear, placing it to his heart and forcing himself upon it, all before Dalric could react.

"What price?" Dalric demanded, holding the old man's face above the water, as he drifted towards death. "What price?" he insisted, shaking the old man as if he were just sleeping, but the old man spoke no more.

Stromgalee lunged at the first figure that materialised from the reeds. A young woman, who effortlessly died, silently on the end of his spear. A man, be it her husband or her lover, launched himself onto his back, bashing at his head blindly with a rock, incensed by the sight of his woman, laying dead in the mud. His attack was so rabid and disorganised that he did no more than scrape the skin from the side of Stromgalee's head, before he was thrown to the floor and brutally killed with a single blow from the raider lord's axe.

For all of the chaos of his surroundings, Stromgalee stopped for a second, his attention drawn by the scene that laid by his feet. The young couple laid, almost touching, their contorted and bloodied bodies partially submerged in marsh water. He pulled his spear from the stomach of the woman, allowing her body to settle to a more natural position. He reached down and gently took her hand, carefully placing it in the hand of her lover. "May the spirits keep you as one," he uttered, before turning to rejoin the battle.

"Back to the village," he shouted as the screams and battle cries of both his men and the villagers seemed to increase to a constant, haunting screech, only muffled by the lashing rain. "Back to the village I say," he commanded, hurling his spear through the reeds, at an attacking villager, adding another blood chilling scream to the collective shriek of the battle, as the man fell into a motionless heap.

"We fight them at the village," he yelled more desperately, as his blindness to the battle around him caused him to panic. Only as he began to hear men splashing though the water, towards the dryer land of Fengate did he begin to withdraw from the battlefield himself. Little did he know, but he was one of the last to leave the slaughter of the reed-beds. Be it his loyalty to his men, or stubborn pride, he would never allow himself to be the first to safety.

"Gather at the village," he called as the reeds cleared and a number of his men came into view, hurriedly running from the confusion and death of the marshes. Still partially obscured by reeds, Stromgalee stopped, to call back, hoping there were still men to emerge. He began to count the men he could see, as they reached the slightly higher ground of the village. He uttered a silent plea to the Sun God, for there to be more survivors to come, but as the words left his lips, one of his men fell to the floor with an arrow in his back.

He drew his sword, looking back into the reeds for someone to fight, settling in the end to take a rage induced swipe at a particularly heavy pulse of rain. He looked back to the village, prompted by a fresh cry of fury. As he did so, more than twenty spear wielding Alluni and Estranians stepped from cover and hurled their weapons at his surviving men. These were different; warriors, every one of them. Almost every spear hit its target, each of his remaining men dying within a few seconds of each other.

Stromgalee put his hand over his eyes, in the hope of making what he was seeing less real, only to be struck by the same horror, when he moved his hand again. Fuelled by a destructive rage and shock, he lashed out at the reeds behind him. The rain suddenly eased. The cries suddenly stopped. His world had, in a breath, collapsed.

He composed himself enough to return to the cover of the thicker reeds. He constantly looked back, struck by the sudden silence, taking it as a sign that his men were all dead. He leapt back in uncharacteristic fear, as one of his own men appeared in front of him; his face entirely smothered in blood.

"I have you," Stromgalee assured him as he took the man's weight in his arms. It was the superstitious man, who had dared to voice his concerns, back at the roundhouse. He was troubled by his inability to speak. His mouth opened, only for blood to dribble from the corners of his mouth. Stromgalee looked over the injured man's shoulder as he hung in his arms. His back had been slashed so deeply that the wound hung wide open, exposing the white of a shoulder blade.

The man gripped his tunic and pulled him closer, once more opening his mouth in the hope of speaking. "Curse you, Lord," he eventually uttered, collapsing entirely, as if he were at peace for having said what he needed to.

Dead or alive, Stromgalee dropped him into the shallow marsh water, and continued. By now he took every movement and sound to be an enemy. Distant thunder continued to crash, at last convincing him that the raid was indeed cursed.

He stopped to gain some sense of direction. There was no path in front, only more of the same. Paranoia ruled his thinking. He focused his eyes on a faint movement ahead, to the point that he didn't even notice the movement by his feet. He struck out with his leg, as he felt the smarting of an injury to his lower leg, for a moment taking it as an animal bite.

Only as Maldred struck a second time, plunging his dagger deep into his calf muscle, did Stromgalee understand what was happening to him. He fell to the floor, before he could even swing his sword. Again and again Maldred plunged his dagger into whatever flesh he could reach, reddening the mud and reeds with every slash, and rendering the raider lord just another casualty of battle.

With Stromgalee dead, the people of Fengate and Norsea began to emerge. There were some missing, and there were those who mourned them, but the two peoples emerged, bonded by the blood of their mutual enemy.

Awaiting them, standing, as an unblemished fighting force, were the twenty Alluni and Estranian warriors, in full war paint. Elric approached, to greet them as friends, but fully aware they were an aggressive and hostile people. "You have our gratitude," he exclaimed, holding his hands out in welcome.

"We don't require your gratitude," their leader replied with a voice filled with hate and contempt. "Only your obedience."

"We are independent villages... Though we welcome you, we swear no allegiance, not to anyone."

The Alluni commander stepped forwards with his warriors, pulling there spears from the bodies of Stromgalee's men. One man was hanging on to life, even after the spear was yanked from his dying body. Be it for show or fun, the Alluni leader stabbed him in the eye with a thin bladed dagger, bringing swift, but gruesome death.

"You will remain independent, for now," the commander declared, as if entirely in charge. "Independent of us, and independent of each other. There will be no Chiefdom of the marshes. None at all!"

Elric stared him in the hawkish eye, before looking back at his exhausted and bedraggled people, who were still emerging from the marsh. Not one of them looked able to do any more than catch the sharp end of a spear; both physically and mentally drained. "We have no such plans," Elric eventually announced, after a lengthy pause, which inspired the Alluni warriors to present their spears, in readiness for attack.

"Know this, swamp rats. We are twenty men, no more than a hunting party, to keep you children from misbehaving. There are more than four hundred of our like, and we would crush the lot of you, like the lice that you are," their leader announced, not to Elric, but directly to the people.

Not a word was spoken, but fresh from winning a battle that should have been lost, they looked back collectively, without blinking.

"Which one of you is called True Spear?" the Alluni leader demanded angrily, frustrated by the people's apparent defiance.

"There is no such person here," Eldwan replied, taking a step forwards to be heard.

"The True Spear is an outlaw... Anyone found under the same roof will be put to death, beside him."

"The True Spear is an escaped slave... We'd be grateful if you were able to return him, should you stumble across him, on your way home," Elric said smugly, and just as defiantly as he dare.

As quickly as they had appeared, the alliance of Alluni and Estranians vanished back into the plentiful cover of the marshes, their bond never more obvious. They went with a story to tell, of a defiant people, and of deadly outlaw, who's reputation was expanding beyond that of any mortal man.

The moment the warriors had gone, Andura ran from the marsh, weaving through the still smouldering remains of burnt huts, boats and fish traps. She single mindedly sprinted to the Thane's sacred roundhouse. It was as it had never been before; stacked out with the belongings of the village, and, as had been the hope, they had been left undamaged. The fire was entirely doused, something widely believed to curse a village. Not even a smouldering ember was left, such was the thorough and purposeful nature of Stromgalee's act of spiritual vandalism.

Andura tentatively moved to the back of the house, amongst the piles of furs, and jars of corn. She lifted a still damp hide, to release a promising puff of smoke. She tittered with joy, before blowing repeatedly, upon the smouldering pot of pig fat. "We still have the fire... The fire of our fathers lives on," she called to the handful of people whom had gathered behind her, most prominently, her father, Elric.

The word of the seer's death shocked the people of Fengate and Norsea, as if he were there own family. He was ceremonially returned to the village, in a procession led by Elaina. She chanted the many praises to the spirits as twenty or so people led his carriers through the marsh, back to the village.

Despite him being her only family, in the village, and her life long guide, Elaina never shed a tear. It would have been a sign of weakness that just couldn't be, for the great priestess that she must become.

So many families had lost someone, some had lost their homes, while others were nursing wounds that were not likely to heal, yet every one of them stopped and knelt, in honour of the wisdom of the man, as the seer's body slowly passed them.

His body was returned to his roundhouse. A place where his body could be laid to receive the honours of the living, before being sent forwards to the eternal grasp of the dead. Even as he was being presented on a wooden table, for visitors, people began to gather, and spiritual chants echoed around the village, in an almost ghostly manner. Garlands of flowers were rested against the wall of the house, and flower petals sprinkled on the ground.

Elaina knelt for a moment, uttering words to her dead grandfather's lifeless body. These weren't the enchantments that those nearby may have assumed, but words of affection, to her grandfather. Only then, as the house was emptied did she allow herself to shed a single, lone tear. That tear was the fruit of not only her loss, but also the weight of responsibility she now carried, in such a turbulent time.

Chapter 16

Only an hour had passed. People were tending to wounds, and seeking out their property, which had been hidden, not only in the Thane's house but in many locations in the surrounding marshes.

The sight of Isena, running frantically towards the village, followed by a Norsean woman, gained the attention of anyone that saw them. It was an inevitable sign that their troubles were far from over. She blundered through the marsh, with her dress pulled up above the knees, splashing through deeper water, as if she was being chased.

"What is it, woman," Elric asked as he steadied her.

"He has the children," she gasped, fighting free of his grip, as if she was frightened to stop. "He has the children," she repeated, pushing forwards, passed Elric; her eyes scanning the village madly, hopelessly looking for any sign of them.

"The raider is dead," Elric insisted. "Who has them?"

"The Three... Colos The Three has them," she yelled back at him, while the second woman ran to her husband, hysterically sobbing for help. Elric took from her hand the emblem of Hathpit; a gulls foot, with three of the birds wing feathers bound to it. It was as good as a signature.

Eldwan happened to be the nearest man to Hob and Alhart. He swiftly turned his spear to Hob, just because he was closest. In turn, Alhart drew his bow back, holding a careful aim upon Eldwan.

"Walk backwards," he whispered to Hob.

"We didn't fight for Colos... We fought along side you, on the instruction of Vintnor, the True Spear," Alhart exclaimed as the two paced, tensely, back into the cover of the reeds. "Don't ask me why," he uttered as an afterthought, before running frantically, to gain as much of a head start on Elric's people as possible.

"Every man and woman who can walk or hold a weapon," Elric declared. "We go to Hathpit."

To Dugan's amazement, Andura smiled. "What is it?" he asked, puzzled by her joy.

"He'll definitely come back. I just know it now," she bubbled, delighted by the workings of her own mind.

Dugan grinned back at her, just because she was talking to him, but he really didn't understand what she was talking about.

They were, just as Colos had hoped, a beaten and battered people, as they made their way to Hathpit. There was no military order to them; no organisation or plan, as there had been, when they took on stromgalee. They were now just an outraged people, with little more than blood to put forward.

Elaina was the last to leave the village. To leave her grandfather's body unattended seemed so wrong, yet she knew she must. Only five people were visible in the village as she left; all injured. Everyone else was ahead, making there way through the marsh, not on a single path, but spread out, over a wide area, to avoid ambush.

She made her way, with her mind far from the there and then. Memories of her youth came to mind, before she joined her grandfather in Fengate. She remembered carefree times, without responsibility, and harsher times too. Soon her thinking moved to the future, to the weight of responsibility her new role would bring, and how much people would look to her for guidance, yet, at heart, she felt unguided herself.

"Has our priestess lost her way?" came the voice of Dalric, standing boldly in front of her. "Now, you see, I told you the old man wouldn't live forever, didn't I... I must be a seer!" he jeered.

Elaina stood upright and defiant, as he approached her, not allowing herself to be lowered by hollow words of hate. "I think it's time we had some spiritual time," he uttered, as he touched, just with one finger, the front of her blood spattered, white dress.

She did not react, even as he gripped the cloth in his hands. She just stared deep into his lustful and perverted eyes. He ripped the front of the dress wide open, exposing both of breasts, right down to a tuft of ginger pubic hair.

"Enjoying yourself yet? Can you feel the blood pumping through your limp prick?" she asked calmly, still without reacting to his actions, or her own nudity. "Well, have a good look, that should do it for you," she said, sliding out of the dress entirely.

Dalric gripped his groin, to feel himself entirely impotent.

"What have you done, Witch?"

"You asked a question of the seer, now the seer is giving you your answer... That is the price you pay for the power you will one day wield."

Dalric stood, shocked, upon the receiving end of the Seer's power. He staggered back, yelling in despair, while Elaina slid her dress back onto her shoulders, tying a string of sedge around her waist to hold it in place.

"Witch," He screamed at the top of his voice as she casually walked away, as if nothing had happened, leaving him to his despair.

The rest of the villagers reached Hathpit, without interference. The very purpose of taking the children was to bring Elric's people to his feet. Though he would have been happy to vanquish them in battle, the greater prize was to rule them.

The eight children were tethered to posts, near the Thane's roundhouse. They were prominently displayed, offering no chance for them to be quietly released, under the imminent fall of darkness.

Colos himself sat upon his throne of furs, overlooking his captives, proudly, as if they were each of them fearsome warriors. He waiting for Elric. He knew he had to come, and he knew that when he did, he would have the upper hand.

As Elric, and the weary and injured people of Fengate and Norsea entered the village, they found themselves surrounded by heavily armed men and women, but it wasn't the weapons that offered such a threat. It was the freshness of the warriors. They were sharp and on edge. Their reflexes were at their zenith and they stood both strong, and without injury.

The Hathpit warriors mingled amongst them as Elric led his people to face Colos. They neither threatened, nor spoke. Just their presence was enough to confirm in the minds of every person present, that if it came to a fight, Fengate and Norsea was done.

"It has been some time since we had a neighbourly visit," Colos declared cheerfully, stroking the handle of his ceremonial sword, which laid beside him, for effect, rather than him having any practical use for it.

"Thane Colos. You have my gratitude for taking care of our children, in a time of danger. We will be glad to replace any food they may have eaten, during their stay," Elric exclaimed, to the amusement of the people of Hathpit.

"It has been entirely my pleasure," Colos declared, holding his arms out, to be helped up. "It only goes to prove the importance of our humble villages standing as one, under one great and powerful leader, for the good of us all... Only then can the raiders be kept at bay."

Elric paid his words little attention, instead reaching down to cut free the nearest of the children. Colos only had to shake his over sized head, for a man to put a spear edge to Elric's throat. "Thing is this, Elric The Pig, such an alliance has to agree upon one great and powerful leader, and, well you don't look all that powerful, right now."

Elric stood on tiptoes, to relieve the pressure of the blade from his throat, quickly dropping his knife. He looked around the crowd, seeing Hob and Alhart amongst the Hathpit people and his own battle weary people, being slowly surrounded by the Hathpit guard.

"United, the villages of the marshes will become a great chiefdom. Is there any man here who would doubt that?" Colos demanded menacingly, as his most loyal warriors moved amongst Elric's people. A man began to prod one of the tethered children with the tip of his spear, just to intimidate the adults. "Any man at all?"

Andura handed Dugan her sword, and began to move towards the Hathpit dominated side of the gathering. She recognised Evali and those who had fought with Vintnor, who mingled amongst their people, as returning heroes. Colos' favourable situation had earned them redemption in his eyes.

She held her hands out from her side, to demonstrate her lack of a weapon. Every step she took, felt like it could be her last. She struggled to contain her erratic breathing, as the fear overcame her. With every person she passed, and every hand that reached out, she felt further from her own people, as if she were sinking in a bottomless pit. The touching hands quickly began to grab, nipping and squeezing, tearing her dress and pulling her hair. The wall of people surrounded her crushing and menacing, stripping her of her clothes clawing at her flesh, not in a sexual manner, but as a pack of wolves engulf a dying animal.

Colos had stopped speaking, just to watch the show, delighting in Elric's misery. "A strong and powerful leader, A true chief, could stop that," Colos declared as Elric was restrained by a second guard.

"Then do it. Control your people," Elric yelled, struggling hopelessly to free himself.

Through the increasingly chaotic crowd, the screams of Dugan became the loudest; first as he fought to reach Andura, then, as a guard's spear was plunged into his back, removing her most loyal friend from view.

Only as sections of Andura's blood spattered dress were being thrown around the rabid mob, and Elric was at a point of despair, did Colos point to the ground by his feet, requiring Elric to kneel.

Andura laid huddled in a defensive ball, awaiting death. Her skin was being scratched with fingernails and prodded, solely for the purpose of causing pain. They stamped on her legs, but never her head, the primary goal being to make her suffer for as long as possible.

She drifted in and out of consciousness. The pain was no longer clear to her, as her senses struggled to understand its intensity. Through her half closed eye, she became aware of light. It was something that could have easily been mistaken for spiritual intervention; the Sun God himself perhaps.

She struggled to hold the eye open long enough to achieve focus, allowing a picture to slowly come into view. Evali stood above her, with two of the other warriors who had fought with Vintnor, holding the tip of her spear to a randomly selected throat.

Colos held his hand up, to stop the beating, only after Evali's intervention, but he was happy that the order appeared to be his. He had achieved his dream. Elric was on the floor, by his feet, acknowledging him to be the first chief of the marshes.

"My people," he declared, standing as proudly as the weight of his immense frame would allow. "We have together repelled the brutality of the raiders. We have sent the Alluni running in fear, and that is just the beginning... Under my divine leadership, each of you will see wealth and victory in equal measure." Colos took his magnificently crafted sword and held it high above his head, before lowering it quickly, the weight of the metal, combined with his fat laden arm, being just too heavy to hold for long.

"For such great victories, a truly great gratitude needs to be made to the Sun God," he announced, once more raising the sword, this time just to shoulder height.

Elric remained still. He awaited his execution, not with fear, but a sense of relief. He had faced hopelessness, time and time again, in the past days. The attack on Andura was the final straw to him; a point at which a swift end, carried an appeal.

The people of Fengate looked on in horror, as could be expected, but the fall of expectant silence, was shared by all. Colos smirked as he drew the sword higher, ready to strike.

A collective gasp swept through the people, shocked by the sudden death by spear, of the guard, standing by Colos' side. Colos dropped the sword as a nervous reflex, not of a warrior, but a coward. "Guards. To you Thane... Protect your Thane," he yelled, turning, looking into the fading light, to those around him, crippled by fear.

The guard had been so perfectly struck down, as if from nowhere, yet Colos knew he would have been the easier target. The words True Spear were being uttered across the crowd and weapons were being readied. Whispering and movement began as people who, only moments before, thought they knew which side they were on, considered their options.

The second guard lunged with his sword, as Elric scrambled to his feet. It had been a delayed reaction, stalled by doubt and confusion. The silent passing of the blade through the air, was swiftly halted by the thud of spear on flesh, knocking the second guard backwards, soundly dead.

For the first time in so long, Colos stood alone and vulnerable. "Protect your Thane," he called with increasing desperation, his eyes flitting from place to place, looking into the dim twilight for those who would stand in his defence.

Elric stood, first on his feet, then on a stack of thatch. "The True Spear did not strike your Thane down, because it was not his place... Be you of Hathpit, of Norsea or of Fengate, you have earned the right to choose your leader and the life you'd lead, or indeed the death you'd suffer." He was careful to look directly at not only those of Fengate and Norsea as he spoke, but also to the people of Hathpit.

Colos shouted wildly, demanding his death, but for the first time, nobody listened. He stood alone; his extreme obesity leaving him at the mercy of anyone who would do him harm.

The crowd absorbed Elric's words, accepting them as wisdom. "You, the people of Hathpit must choose," he continued, only after seeing Isena tending to Andura's wounds. "Choose your old leader if you are happy with the life you've lived so far; with the man he is... You could choose a Thane from amongst your own number, and hope the raiders don't come back, or maybe, on this day blessed by all of the spirits, and smiled upon by the Sun God himself, you could choose a Chief, who would allow us to defend our lands, side by side."

Cheers and words of agreement reverberated across the crowd, but Elric's focus was on one insignificant looking figure, who stood in the shadows of the many flames that were being ignited as the last vestiges of daylight fizzled into darkness. He couldn't make out a face, but the fact the figure was leaving the crowd, highlighted him to Elric. He wore a cloth hood and seemed to be deliberately looking away from anyone he met.

Elric continued to speak to the people, but he looked continuously to the mysterious figure, following him with a fixed stare, until he was lost from sight.

In a matter of a minute, the tables had turned on Colos. Eventually, alone and afraid, he began to reach for his sword, stumbling as he attempted to pick it up, without falling to the floor. Elric briefly rolled his eyes towards him, before looking back to his crowd, showing only contempt for his old adversary.

Even as Colos gripped his sword, Elric continued to speak, his faith being placed entirely in the hands of those around him. He could see in the faces of those in front of him, that Colos was preparing to strike.

The concerned faces of so many people, glowed and flickered in the torch light. Time seemed to slow, as he selected his words, knowing they could be his last, yet still he resisted making any physical action to defend himself.

With his loathed enemy in striking distance, and the chiefdom within his grasp, Colos' frailty seemed so much less. He gripped his sword with both hands and stepped forwards, swinging the sword in a broad arc. At that final, decisive moment, several of the people of Fengate lurched to Elric's aid, but were either too far, or were blocked by those still loyal to Colos.

Idenica of Norsea, propelled herself wildly, over the shoulders of the two women in front of her, blundering hopelessly to the ground. She scrambled forwards, prepared to stop the blade with her own body.

Eventually, when the shock of those in front of him allowed him to ignore the danger no more, Elric turned. Idenica, a woman of Norsea, stood, grasping with both hands the sword arm of the oversized dictator. Colos offered no resistance. He froze; a look of shock, dominating his face as he stared, horrified, at Elric. After a few seconds, he dropped to his knees, and then face down, dead, with his own ornately carved dagger, thrust deep into his back. Behind him, with bloodied hands, stood his young wife, Edrana, of Hathpit.

Chapter 17

Much had changed in three days. An elaborate funeral ceremony was arranged for the old Seer, with many of the people of Hathpit and Norsea attending the impressive funeral pyre. It was an event that cemented the new alliance, seeing the three peoples mingling as one community.

The proceedings went on late into the night as the sparks and smoke transported the old man to a new dimension, where he would be at one with the spirits; an honour reserved only for the most holy of men.

As Priestess, Eleena carried out her duties without emotion, in the manner she knew her grandfather would expect of her. She had in those three days, not only filled the void, the death of the old man had made, in the lives of the people of Fengate, but she had also become a rudder for the still shaken peoples of Norsea and Hathpit.

On the third night, as the smoke and occasional sparks still blew in the keen wind, from the funeral fire, Vintnor dared to return. It wasn't an announced visit. He had set his mind upon leaving, and never looking back, yet his heart and soul needed a degree of closure, before he could move on.

He watched from the reeds, listening to the voices resonating through the darkness of night. Despite such losses, and even after such a high ranking funeral, the village seemed to carry a certain joy, which he'd not seen there before.

He smiled to hear the loud, but simple voice of Dugan, booming from Eldwan's roundhouse. Vintnor had seen him fall to a spear, in the defence of Andura, and he'd assumed him dead.

At the pile of smouldering ash, a single figure knelt, silhouetted against the glow, both of the fire, and the countless stars of that clearest of nights. He approached boldly, knowing that another stranger in the village wouldn't be noticed.

He considered his words as he knelt down beside her. She was no longer to be treated as an ordinary woman. She was now entirely spiritual; a person to be treated with the uttermost respect. "There's a good few of them come to see him off," he suddenly blurted, pointing to the stars.

"The spirits welcome him as one of their own," she said, without breaking her stare upon the smouldering ash.

Two more minutes passed before another word was spoken, and then it was only an appeal to the spirits, uttered under her breath as she suddenly stood, brandishing a long handled wooden spoon. She reached into the ashes, focused upon one specific point. With great concentration, she picked from the ash a small shard of bone, which she dropped into a waiting earthen jar.

For once, even Vintnor knew better than to ask. Over the next five minutes, sections of scull and thigh bone were added, as well as an entire finger, which had escaped the worst of the heat. Only as she sealed the jar with the tight fitting wooden stopper, did she speak. "My grandfather, the greatest of holy men will one day reside in our most holy ground. Until that day I will keep him safe, as he will keep me."

Vintnor nodded solemnly, before rising to his feet, at last feeling too uncomfortable to stay any longer. "Do you not ask after her?" she called, as he walked away.

"Andura?"

"Of course. That is what's on your mind isn't it?" she replied, for the first time facing him, and entirely focused upon him.

"I know of her poor health," he replied. "I have friends who've seen her."

"Not how she is. The now is only a point in a journey... Would you not know of her journey?"

"What do you know?" he asked, with suspicion that there was a story to tell, and foreboding as to its detail.

"Ask me a question... The question is half of the answer." It was a statement that could have come from the old seer himself; cryptic, yet with a suggestion of great wisdom.

"What will she be to me?" he asked, after a considerable pause for thought.

Eleena stepped towards him. She brutally gripped his jaw and turned his head to an angle, which allowed the light from the rising moon to reflect from his eyes. "She will be the twine that binds you. The master that will never free you from your bond. She will hold you back, to your dying breath, and all the time you will feel her weight dragging heavy on your heart... She will never truly be yours, but you will be forever hers."

Vintnor stepped back; not shaken, or disturbed by her prophesy, as was the usual reaction of the devout villagers. He smiled broadly. "Sounds like fun," he joked, before turning towards Elric's roundhouse, with a single, deluded notion, occupying his mind.

"Vintnor," she called, in an entirely different tone. "Maldred!" she said, by means of a warning.

He just looked back and grinned. It didn't mean he didn't take her warning seriously, but he had received warnings from all directions, since his arrival in Fengate and he'd found the best way of handling them, was to entirely ignore them.

For a while he lurked in the darkness, outside Elric's roundhouse. He listened to the voices inside, slowly gauging who was present, and even their locations within the house. Ultimately, there was only so much waiting his patience could bear. He pulled the cloth hood over his head and quietly ducked beneath the door curtain. People had been coming and going all even, and he hoped one more figure in the shadows of the outer wall might not be spotted.

The very second he entered the building, he made eye contact with Isena, who sat, weaving by the firelight. She didn't make any physical reaction at first, she just maintained a stare, which fixed him to the spot.

Idenica sat by her side, tending a spit of meat, unaware of the stranger's identity. "We owe you some gratitude," Isena eventually declared, having carefully considered her options. "You have done much for our united peoples." Her words had been crafted in those moments of silence, to appease Idenica, and to see Vintnor gone in the shortest possible time. She took the stick of meat from Idenica's hand and presented it to him as if it were a considerable reward. "I know my daughter would have liked to thank you herself, but she is with her new husband, on the Norsea side tonight." She made eye contact with Idenica, as if to signal the purpose of her words.

She turned Vintnor around, physically guiding and pushing him from the doorway. "We wouldn't want you waking our other guest, would we," she said, looking back anxiously, to Maldred, who laid, curled up amongst a pile of furs, against the back wall of the house.

"She is married?" he asked, taken aback by her words.

"She's only ever had eyes for him," she said, looking back to Idenica as she joined them outside. "Now you must be going, before my husband comes back. As our new chieftain, he would be under pressure to turn you over to the Alluni."

Vintnor couldn't find the words to reply. There was nothing to say, Isena had said it all. He just pulled his hood back around his face and walked from the village, without speaking another word.

"Who was that, mother?" Andura asked, as she rolled from beneath her furs, her bruised and scratched face glowing in the firelight.

"Just one of the Hathpit lot. Looking for your father. I saw him off, you never know what they are wanting," she complained, smiling to Idenica, and proud of her own deceit. "You get some sleep, my dear. You've much healing to do before your wedding."

Walking from the village, Vintnor considered what had just happened, and he also recalled both the old Seer's words, and Eleena's, and he promptly dismissed them as nonsense. At that moment in time, he simply couldn't see any circumstance in which he would return to those villages, which had shown him nothing but trouble, and promised him only death.

The morning saw Elric's return from Hathpit, where he had spent the night, purposely and symbolically embracing it as his home. In many ways he was a changed man, outwardly at least. He demonstrated a love and fear of the spirits and the Sun God, in equal measure. The people of Hathpit were particularly devout. Their fear of the unseen forces had been used as a tie to bind them by Colos, who had always claimed to be born of the spirits.

Once out of public view, he joined his wife by the fire, as he had always done. He looked back at Andura, who sat propped against the back wall, supping soup. "You look so much better today," he said, but the look of pity on his face told a different story, as the fire illuminated her battered face.

"She's walked a few steps this morning," Isena said enthusiastically, as she continued about her tasks.

"Is he really going?" Elric asked. "Not that I'm complaining," he added promptly.

"Why don't you ask him to stay?"

"A man has his pride. He might yet live well on his boat," Elric argued, being keen to see his house free of Maldred, having quietly and privately dubbed him Maldred the miserable.

Maldred's boat was one of those left behind as the remains of Stromgalee's men retreated. It was a sizeable boat, but could be sailed by one able bodied man, if the need arose, though Maldred was so far from able bodied.

"We found a few of your spears, for trading," Isena explained, as he dragged himself onto the boat. "I wish it were more, but we may well need every weapon, ourselves."

"You have been more than kind," Maldred declared. "You both have."

Isena laid a leather sack of food, on the edge of his boat. "For your strength," she declared, as Elric promptly pushed his boat from the mooring.

"May the Sun God keep you all," Maldred shouted, whilst awkwardly guiding his vessel through the narrow channel, to the open river.

"Spirits be with you," Elric half-heartedly mumbled, his interest consumed but a broken post on the mooring.

It wasn't until he was on open water, and well away from Fengate that Maldred assessed his remaining wealth. Six spears laid across the floor of the boat. Not the best by any means; mainly damaged from battle. They represented an offering from Elric's people, so they hadn't sent him away with nothing. A handful of used arrows, laid amongst them, but no bow, which caused him to huff at their lack of thought.

He pulled up his sleeve, right to the shoulder, to assess his true wealth. There, clenched to his flesh, were eight rings of crafted gold. It was a wealth that made him so much more than a man drifting to his death, as was the assumption of the people of Fengate. It was more than food and shelter. Unlikely as it seemed, he had a life ahead of him.

With Stromgalee dead, his remaining men ran. With the Alluni actively involved, any plan for revenge was abandoned, and any order amongst them, lost to the weak leadership of Ruke. They began to disperse, only to be driven together again by an Estranian attack, forcing them back to the river, where they were trapped and at the mercy of both the Estranians and the small force of Alluni, who had fought at Fengate.

Ruke rallied his men as best he could, but he was a thug, not a leader, and certainly not a thinking man. Three men began to swim, prompting him to angrily hurl a spear at one of them; effectively discarding his only remaining weapon.

Only as death seemed imminent, did forgotten hope appear, in the form of Balmoor, skilfully sailing three boats up the river. It was an act that would not be forgotten. It gave him credibility then, and in the times that were to follow. He was to those desperate men, now an equal, if not more than an equal. More than that, he was a hero, protected from those whom might see him as a future threat.

Hiam had been with Ruke's group. As was the way of the man, when things started to go wrong, he went his own way, running from the danger, his cowardliness being his most powerful instinct.

He was neither a skilled marshman, nor a physically gifted man, and as such he was soon found by the Estranians, skulking in a disused fox burrow.

One skill he did excel in was that of grovelling and begging. He came close to being killed, but after declaring his undying loyalty to the Alluni, and spinning a tale of his own abduction, he was allowed to live.

He was the slimiest of men, manipulating the trust of the Estranian Captain, to the point that the two walked side by side for the last miles to the Alluni war camp; their topic of conversation being entirely focused upon tactics of attacking the newly formed chiefdom of the marshes.

i

Printed in Dunstable, United Kingdom